JACKING

I tapped keys, and Doc Lee's face came up on the screen.

"We've talked it over," he said, "and we've decided to trust you. We'll give you the full schematics for the project. If you'll jack on line, we can feed everything right in, and you can see if you have any questions."

I should have stopped to consider that, but I didn't. I just nodded and jacked in and said, "Ready."

I got the initial feed, good hard data on Epimetheus, Nightside City, the vectors needed to stop the city—and then they cut my body out of the circuit but left me hooked into the system with no way to move my hand and unplug.

The bastards knew just what they were doing. They had me on an indefinite hold awaiting data transmission, and of course they weren't sending any transmission.

I sat like that, staring at the gigo on the screen, for maybe ten minutes; then the door buzzed as somebody ran an override on it. It opened, and the muscle came in...

By Lawrence Watt-Evans
Published by Ballantine Books:

THE LORDS OF DÛS
    The Lure of the Basilisk
    The Seven Altars of Dûsarra
    The Sword of Bheleu
    The Book of Silence

The Misenchanted Sword

With a Single Spell

The Cyborg and the Sorcerers

The Wizard and the War Machine

Nightside City

NIGHTSIDE CITY

CITY

Lawrence Watt-Evans

A Del Rey Book

BALLANTINE BOOKS • NEW YORK

Dedicated to
Dr. Sheridan Simon,
who designed Epimetheus and the Eta Cass system to
my specifications—
and also dedicated to the memories of
Jim Morrison
and
Humphrey Bogart

Chapter One

THE CITY OUTSIDE MY WINDOW WAS A CACOPHONY OF neon and stardust, a maze of blinding glitter and flash, and from where I sat it was all meaningless, no discrete images at all—nothing discrete, and certainly no discretion. I knew that the casino ads were shimmying and singing like sirens, luring passersby onto the rocks of the roulette wheels and randomizers, sucking them in with erotic promises of riches, but all that reached me through the window was a tangle of colored light and a distant hum, punctuated every so often by the buzz and blink of a macroscopic floater passing nearby. Even the big ships landing or lifting didn't bother me—the window was angled so I couldn't see them unless they buzzed the Trap, which would have gotten any pilot's license erased, and the port's big damper fields kept the noise out of the city.

As long as I kept the window transparent I always had the flicker and the sparkle and the hum for a background, and the blaze of light and color was there if I bothered to look, but I didn't have the noise and flash grinding in on me.

I liked it that way. There was a time when I'd had an office in the Trap, as we called it—the Tourist Trap—but that was a long time ago. When the case I'm telling you about came up I had my little place in the burbs, on Juarez Street, and I could see the lights of Trap Over all the more clearly for the added distance. Instead of the overwhelming come-ons, the holos and the shifting sculptures of stardust, all I saw was just light and noise.

And was it ever really anything more?

Of course, I won't lie to you—I wasn't out in the burbs by choice, not really. When I was young and stupid and new at my work I fell for a sob story while I was on a casino job, and I let a welsher take an extra day. He was off-planet within an hour, and IRC had to shell out the bucks to put an unscheduled, shielded call through to Prometheus and nail him there. They weren't happy with me, and when Interstellar Resorts Corporation isn't happy with you, you don't work in the Trap. Even their competitors don't argue with that.

I'm just glad the bastard didn't have enough cash to buy his way out-system; if IRC had had to chase him to Sol or Fomalhaut or somewhere, I'd have been lucky to live a week.

Of course, if he'd had out-system fare he would have paid his tab in the first place. It wasn't that big, which was another reason I'm still up and running.

When you can't work in the Trap, though, there isn't that much detective work left on Epimetheus, short of security work in the mines. I wasn't ready to fry my genes out there in some corner of nightside hell, making sure some poor jerk who didn't know any better didn't pocket a few kilocredits' worth of hot ore. Mine work might have had more of a future than anything in the city, but it's not the sort of future I'd care to look forward to.

And I didn't know anything but detective work, and besides, I wasn't going to give IRC the satisfaction of driving me out of business.

That left the burbs, from the Trap to the crater's rim, so that's where I went. It's all still part of the city, really—everything inside the crater wall is Nightside City, and anything outside in the wind, or off Epimetheus, isn't, which keeps it simple. So I was still in the city, and I figured I could pick up the crumbs, the jobs that the Trap detectives didn't want, and get by on that.

Sometimes it worked, sometimes it didn't. I worked cheap and I made sure everyone knew that. I got my office out in Westside, where you could almost see the sun peeping over the eastern rim, where the land was cheap because it would be the first to fry as the dawn broke. I was only on Juarez, though; I wasn't all the way out in the West End. I stayed as close in as I thought I could afford, to buy myself time. Eastside, in the crater wall's shadow, would be safe for about three years after the West End went—not that I'd care to stay there once the port, over to the south of the Trap, goes—and that meant it was more expensive. I might have found more work out that way, I don't know, but there were too many people out east who knew what IRC thought of me.

In Westside they generally knew, but none of them could afford to care.

One thing about moving out of the Trap—I moved right out of my social life, too. My friends at the casinos somehow never found the time to call me anymore. I didn't meet any tourists out on Juarez, either. The people I did meet—well, some of them weren't bad, but they weren't exactly high society.

Besides, I had to work so hard to survive I didn't have

time to hang out in the streets. Most of my business dealings were with clients or with software, and socializing with clients is always a mistake.

I don't see anything wrong with socializing with software, as far as it goes, but it tends to be pretty limited. You don't meet much software that takes the same approach to things like sex, credit, food, or family that humans do. Software doesn't have family in the human sense.

Of course, I didn't have very *much* family. All the family I had left in the city was my brother Sebastian, and he worked in the Trap; he called sometimes, stayed in touch, but he didn't make it a point to drop by, if you know what I mean. His employers might not have been pleased if he had.

We hadn't been all that close anyway. We weren't any closer with me out on Juarez.

I had my office, and I did any work that came my way. I tracked down missing husbands, missing wives, missing children, missing pets—biological, cybernetic, or whatever. I went after missing data and of course, missing money. Anything anyone mislaid I went after, and more often than not I found whatever it was.

I got a break once when I followed up a string of complaints about a crooked operator at the Starshine Palace and nailed a guy so dumb that he was skimming from both the customers *and* the house but who had a really slick way of doing it; catching him was good work, and it got me a lot of good publicity. It also made me an enemy, as the casino had Big Jim Mishima on the case, and I beat him to it, and the casino kept Jim's fee as a result. Big Jim resented that, and I can't blame him, but I couldn't see my way clear to screw up; I had a reputation and damn little else, and I keep what I have. At least, I do when I can.

The Palace almost considered talking to me again after that, since I'd saved them some juice, but then IRC reminded them of the gruesome details of my past and they decided I still wasn't welcome.

But I was less unwelcome at the Palace than in any of the other casinos—like a leftover program wasting memory, but one they might need someday, not pure gritware.

I did a few other jobs here and there—whatever I could get. I ate dinner most days, usually lunch, too, and I never got more than two months behind on my rent or my com bill. Every so often I even splurged on a drink or a sandwich at Lui's Tavern, two blocks over on Y'barra, and watched Lui's holoscreen instead of my own.

Of course, in a year or so I was going to have to go to the mines, move east, or get off-planet if I didn't want terminal sunburn, and it didn't look as if I'd have enough saved up to get off Epimetheus. Moving east didn't have much appeal—it just put off the inevitable. I was beginning to contemplate the inevitability of a career in heavy metals.

My situation was not exactly an endless scroll of delights, and my prospects were a good bit less rosy than the sky I saw behind the Trap. That sky looked a little brighter every day, even when Eta Cass B was out of sight somewhere below the horizon. Which it wasn't, just then, when this case first came up. It was out of sight of my window, but I knew that Eta Cass B was high in the west, and I could see its glow reddening the dark buildings just across the street, while its big brother reddened the eastern horizon and washed half the stars out of the sky above with a blue that looked paler every day.

The sky used to be black, of course, and was still black and spattered with stars in the west, but the first hint of dark blue was starting to creep up from the eastern rim even before I left the Trap, and there were fewer stars to be seen every time I bothered to look.

Every time another star vanished, so did another chunk

of the City's population; anyone who could afford to leave did, and those who couldn't afford it were saving up. That was cutting into what little business I had—I didn't have a single case going, and hadn't for two days. I was sick of watching the vids, and with no income I couldn't afford to go out, not even to Lui's.

So I sat there, watching the glitter and sparkle of the city try to drown out that insidious coming dawn, and I wasn't any too happy about my life. Getting out of the Trap was probably good for my soul—I suppose my ancestors would know for sure; I can only guess—but it wasn't any good for my mood or my credit line. The distance and the window fields kept the city's noise down to a murmur, but I could still hear it, and I was listening to it so hard just then that at first I thought the beep was coming from outside.

Then the com double-beeped, and I knew it wasn't outside. I hit the pad on the desk—the place had had pressure switches when I moved in, and I couldn't afford to convert to voice, so I roughed it. I guess an earlier tenant liked his fingers better than his tongue—or maybe he was some kind of antiquarian fetishist. It wasn't even a codefield, but an actual keypad. Before I took that office I'd never seen one anywhere else except history vids, let alone used one, but I got the hang of it after a while. It gave the place a certain charm, an air of eccentricity that I almost liked. It was also a real pain in the ass to use, no matter how much practice I got, but I couldn't afford to do anything about it.

So when the com double-beeped I hit the ACCEPT key. My background music dimmed away and someone asked, "Carlisle Hsing?"

The voice was young and male and belonged to nobody I knew. I could hear the wind muttering behind him, so I knew he was outside, probably on my doorstep from the sound of it. I didn't bother to check the desk's main screen yet.

"Yeah," I said. "I'm Hsing."

"I—uh, *we* want to hire you."

That sounded promising. I flicked on the screen.

He didn't *look* promising. He was a good three days overdue for a shave—either that, or three days into growing a beard, with a long way to go. His hair hadn't been washed recently, either. He was pale and round-eyed and wore a battered port worksuit, one that hadn't been much when it was new—low-grade issue, built, not grown, and all flat gray with no shift. A cheap com jack under his right ear looked clogged with grease, and I wasn't sure about the workmanship on his eyes. He wasn't anybody I'd seen before, not in my office or in Lui's or on the streets, and sure as hell not in the Trap.

Judging by the view behind him, he was indeed on my doorstep. In my business I do get callers in person, not just over the com.

At least, I got this one in person, and he said he wanted to hire me, so I let his looks go for the moment.

"For what?" I asked.

"Ah . . . it's complicated. Can I come in and explain?"

Well, I wasn't doing much of anything. I'd just finished off the final details on my last case, finding a missing kid who had holed up in Trap Under for a week-long wire binge; the fee hadn't done much more than pay the bills. I couldn't afford to turn down much, so I said, "Yeah," and buzzed the door. I didn't turn on the privacy, though, so it logged in his face, voiceprint, pheromone signature, and all the rest.

Any security door will do all that, but most people don't much care, they just let the data slide; me, in my line of work, I'd cleared it with the landlord and had everything tapped straight into my personal com system. The landlord didn't mind—as I said, I generally paid my rent—so I always knew who I had in my office. If this guy tried anything, I was pretty sure I'd be able to find him.

A few minutes later he inched into the office as nervous as a kid going through his first neuroscan and tried not to stare at me. He wasn't that much more than a kid himself; I guessed him at eighteen, maybe twenty, no more. Maybe twenty-one, if you want to use Terran years.

He looked okay—grubby, but not dangerous—and none of the scanners had beeped, but just in case I had my right hand under the desk, holding my Sony-Remington HG-2. The gun laws on Epimetheus were written by a committee, so they're a mess, complicated as hell, and I never did figure out whether that gun of mine was legal, but I liked it and kept it handy just the same. I'd had it brought in, special, from out-system, as a favor from an old friend—an old friend who somehow hadn't called since I left the Trap, but what the hell, I still had the gun.

Owning it was probably good for a fat fine, but only if somebody made a point of it, and I wasn't about to walk past the port watch with it out. I'd drawn it in public a few times, in the Trap, but casino cops don't hassle anyone who might be a player without a better reason than flashing an illegal weapon. Casino cops can be very good at minding their own business.

"Sit down," I said, and the kid sat, very slowly. I had three chairs and a couch; the chairs were floaters, and he took the couch, which had legs. Cautious, very cautious. The cushions tried to adjust for him, but he kept shifting, and one of the warping fields had burned out long ago, leaving a band a few centimeters wide that stayed stiff and straight as a motherboard and screwed up the whole system.

He didn't seem to be in any hurry to talk. He just looked around the place, everywhere but at me. If his eyes were natural, he wasn't in great shape and might have something eating at his nervous system; if they were replacements, he got rooked. The com jack under his ear obviously hadn't been used in weeks. His worksuit was so worn and patched that the circuitry was showing, and I could see that some leads were cut; it was probably stolen.

I felt sorry for any poor symbiote that had to live in the guy—assuming there was one, which I did not consider certain.

But then, my own symbiote wasn't exactly in an ideal environment for the long term.

"So," I said. "Who are you?"

He gave me a sharp look.

"Why?" he asked.

This was looking worse all the time; I hit some keys I knew he couldn't see—with my left hand, because my right had the gun—and started running the door data through the city's ID bank. "I like to know who I'm working for," I said.

He didn't like that. He gave me a look and a silence.

"If you don't tell me who you are, I don't work," I said.

He hesitated, then gave in. "All right," he said. "My name is Wang. Joe Wang."

I nodded and glanced down at one of the desk's pull-out screens. His name was Zarathustra Pickens. He was about a month short of nineteen years old, Terran time. Born on Prometheus, came in-system to the nightside at sixteen— probably looking for casino work, but it didn't say—and did a few short pieces here and there. Last job, cleaning pseudoplankton out of the city water filters. Got laid off a week earlier when the city brought in a machine that was supposed to do the job. Again. They'd been trying machines on that since I was a girl, and they never worked right—sooner or later the pseudoplankton got into the cleaning machines, same as it got into everything else anywhere near water, and screwed them up. Machines that didn't screw up would cost more than people. An organism that could deal with the situation would probably cost even more and might be dangerous if it got out, since the whole planet lives and breathes off pseudoplankton; it's the only significant source of oxygen on Epimetheus.

It's also mean stuff, meaner than any microorganism that ever evolved on Earth; building a bug that could handle it might take one hell of a lot of doing.

I figured Zar Pickens could probably get his job back in a couple of days, so I didn't hold his unemployment against him.

"All right, Mis' Wang," I said. "What can I do for you?"

He got nervous again. "It's not *me*," he said. "I mean, it's not *just* me."

I'd had about enough of his delays. I wasn't inclined to pry the details out one by one. "Okay," I said. "You tell it your way, whatever it is you have to tell, but let's get on with it, shall we?"

He hesitated a bit, then started telling it.

"I live out by the crater wall," he said, "right out in the West End. It's cheap, y'know?"

Cheap, hell, I guessed it was probably free; at least a dozen big buildings out that way were already abandoned. Even a couple on Juarez were abandoned. The owners didn't figure it was worth the repairs and maintenance when the sun's on the horizon, or maybe even already hitting the top floors, so when a building dropped below code, or the complaints started piling up, they would just ditch it. Good, sound business practice, at least by Epimethean standards.

And whether Pickens had had other reasons or not, that explained why he'd come in person; the com lines in the West End are, shall we politely say, unreliable.

I didn't say anything. I just nodded.

Pickens nodded back. "Right, so I don't bother anybody. None of us do; there's a bunch of us out that way, living cheap, not hurting a damn thing. You understand?"

I nodded again. Squatters were nothing new. When I was a girl they'd had to make do with doorways or alleys in the outer burbs, or caves in the crater wall, but they'd been moving inward for years. Especially in the west.

"Okay, fine," Pickens said. "But then about two weeks back some slick-hair shows up, with this big slab of muscle backing him, and says that he works for the new owner, and the rent's gone up, and we pay it or we get out."

I sat back a little and let the HG-2 drop back in the holster; this was beginning to sound interesting. Interesting, or maybe just dumb. It had to be a con of some kind, but that was so obvious even squatters would see it. I put my hands behind my head and leaned back. "New owner?" I asked.

"That's what he said."

I nodded. "Go on."

Pickens shrugged. "That's about it."

"So what do you want me to do?" I asked.

He looked baffled for a minute. "Come on, Hsing," he said. "What do you *think*? We want you to get rid of the guy, of course!" His voice rose and got ugly. "I mean, what's this new owner crap? Who's buying in the West End? The sun is rising, lady! Nobody's gonna buy land in the West End, so what's this new owner stuff? It's gotta be a rook, but when we called the city, they said he was legit, so we can't call the cops, and we can't just take him out ourselves, because this goddamn new owner would send someone else. We need someone who can get it straight; I mean, we don't have anywhere else to go, and we can't pay this fucker's rent!" He was getting pretty excited, like he was about to jump out of the couch; I straightened up and put my hands back down.

"Then how are you planning to pay my fee?" I asked, and the Sony-Remington was back in my hand but still out of sight.

The question stopped him for a moment, even without the gun showing. He shifted again, settling back down, and the couch rippled as it tried to adjust.

"We took up a collection," he said. "Did it by shares, sort of, and we came up with some bucks. They say you work cheap if you like the job, and I sure hope you like this one, because we couldn't come up with much."

"How much?" I asked.

"Two hundred and five credits," he said. "Maybe a little more, but we can't promise."

Well, that sure as hell wasn't much, but I was interested anyway. As the kid said, who's buying land in the West End? That was just dumb. I figured, same as he did, that most likely somebody had rigged up a little swindle with the city management. That two hundred and five wasn't about to pay my fare off-planet, came the dawn, but it could pay for a dinner or two, and I thought the case might have some interesting aspects to it. For an example, I might be able to collect a reward for turning in a crooked city com-op, or if I decided I didn't need a conscience, I could take a little share of whatever the op was sucking down his chute.

"All right, Mis' Wang," I said. "I'll need a hundred credits up-front, and whatever names and addresses you can give me."

He gawked. I mean, his mouth came open, and he just flat-out gawked at me. "You mean you'll *take* it?" he said.

The kid just had no class at all. I wondered how he'd ever managed to land *any* job, even scraping pseudoplankton, and I was ready to bet that his symbiote had died of neglect or embarrassment, if he'd ever had one at all. I'd had about all I wanted of him. "Yes, Mis' Pickens," I said. "I'll take it."

That was that. He pulled out a transfer card and started reeling off the names and addresses of every squatter this rent collector had gone after, and I put it all into the com. The poor jerk never even noticed that I'd used his right name.

Chapter Two

AFTER I FINALLY GOT ZAR PICKENS OUT OF MY OFFICE, I settled in to think about the kid's story. The com brought the music back up a little, but kept it mellow and meditative, and the images on the big holo stayed abstract.

In my line of work I always found it helped to cultivate a suspicious nature, so I leaned back and looked at whether I could be getting conned or set up or otherwise dumped on.

The whole thing looked like a glitch of some kind. Out there at the base of the western wall, if you stood on tiptoe, you could just about see the sun—assuming you were either wearing goggles or didn't mind burning your retinas. In a year nobody would live there without eyeshades and sunscreen, at the very least; more likely no one would live there at all.

A year, hell—ten weeks would probably do it. There were buildings where the top stories were already catching the sun, and the terminator was moving one hundred and thirty-eight centimeters a day. Everyone knew that.

So who'd buy property there?

Nobody. Ever since it began sinking in that sunrise really was coming, that the city founders a hundred and sixty years back really had been wrong about the planet already being tidelocked, real estate prices had been dropping all over Nightside City, and they'd gone down fastest and furthest in the West End. I guessed that you could buy a building lot—or a building—out there for less than a tourist would pay for a blowjob in the Trap, but you still wouldn't be able to collect enough in rents to make your money back before dawn, because rents were dropping, too, and there were plenty of other cheap places, farther east, like the one I lived in.

So nobody in his right mind would actually buy out there. Even if you got the property free, registering the transfer of title would cost enough to make it a bad investment; legal fees hadn't dropped any.

That left four possibilities, as I saw it.

First, someone wasn't in his right mind. You can never rule that one out completely. The really demented are scarce these days, but there are still a few out there. Maybe some poor aberrant had actually bought that future wasteland.

Second, someone had figured out how to get title to the property for nothing, not even transfer fees, and was trying to squeeze a little money out of it. That was free enterprise in action, but it was also pretty sure to be illegal. I might come out ahead if I could prove something.

Third, nobody had bought anything, but somebody was trying to run a scam of some kind on the squatters, maybe just to collect those rents, maybe to get something else out of them, and had enough pull somewhere to get away with it, or had somehow faked the call to the city. Maybe whoever placed the call for the squatters was getting a cut and had called somewhere else entirely. If that was the story, and I proved it, I could count on two hundred and five credits, but the only way I'd get more than that was if the Eastern Bunny dropped it in my lap, or if an opportunity arose for a little creative blackmail, mild enough that I could live with myself.

Fourth, Pickens—if that was his real name after all—was pulling a scam on me.

I couldn't rule any of those out. That fourth one was the one I liked least, of course, and it seemed pretty goddamn unlikely, but I couldn't rule it out. I couldn't figure any way that anyone could get anything worthwhile out of me, with this story or any other, but I couldn't rule it out. I know there are people out there smarter than I am, and that means there are people out there who could fool me if they wanted to. I couldn't figure out why they'd want to—but like I said, they're smarter than I am.

If it was a con, it was a good one. The story was bizarre enough to get my interest, and there weren't any of the telltale signs of a con—nothing too good to be true, no fat fee in prospect, no prepared explanation.

I decided that if it was a con, it was too damn slick for me, and I might as well fall into it, because it would be worth it to see what the story was. So I would assume it wasn't a con.

That left three choices, and they all hinged on whether or not someone had actually paid for those buildings.

I couldn't find out the whole truth sitting at my desk, but I could get the official story, anyway. I hit my keypad, punched up the Registry of Deeds and ran down the list of addresses.

Of course, any jerk could have done that, and somebody supposedly had, because Zar Pickens had said that someone who worked for the city said the new owner was for real. The name the squatters had gotten was West End Properties, but that didn't mean anything more to me than it had to them; I asked for the full transaction records on every address where a squatter had been hassled.

Just for interest, I also tagged the command to give last-called dates for each property file, while I was at it.

There were eleven properties involved where squatters had been asked for rent. They were scattered in an arc along Wall Street and in a couple of blocks on Western Avenue and Deng Boulevard.

All eleven really had been deeded over to new owners in the last six weeks—nominally to eleven different buyers, but that didn't mean anything.

No one had called up any of the files since the transfers had been made, except for Zar Pickens's own building; that had sold five weeks earlier, and someone had called up the transaction record about two weeks back. That would have been the squatters, checking up.

That transfer said West End Properties, all right.

Somebody really was buying property in the West End, or at least getting it transferred to new ownership. That eliminated another of my options: it wasn't just an attempt to muscle a few credits out of the squatters.

But what the hell *was* it? Was somebody actually paying real money for buildings and lots that were about to turn into baked goods?

I was pretty damn curious by now, and I suddenly thought of something else I was curious about. I punched in for all real estate transactions made in the previous six weeks, called for a graphic display on a city map, and cursed the idiot who had wired the system for pressure instead of voice. I almost plugged myself in, but then decided to hold off. I don't like running on wire.

The records showed fifty or sixty recent deeds. After I dropped out a few scattered foreclosures, gambling losses, and in-family transfers, I had about forty left.

They were all in the West End. They covered just about all of the West End, too.

I extended the time back another week—nothing but foreclosures and gambling losses. An eighth week, nothing. Whatever was going on had started just about six weeks back.

But what was going on?

If someone had figured a way to fake property transfers, why stick to the West End? Why not take a bit here and there, maybe catch someone who could actually pay a decent rent? As I said before, there was abandoned property as far in as my own neighborhood, not just in the West End. The impending dawn was not going to catch anyone by surprise, and people had been pulling out gradually for years—half the people I grew up with, the smart ones, were off-planet, and even some of the dumb ones were out in the mines instead of hanging around the city. So if somebody had a way of stealing land, why go for the worst? Why the West End and not Westside, or the Notch, or somewhere?

Maybe there really was something that made the West End valuable after all, even with the sun coming up. I hadn't figured that in my four options.

That seemed pretty damn unlikely. Anything valuable out there should have been stripped out long ago. Most of the utility lines had been.

Somebody was making those title transfers, though, ostensibly buying up property. The next step seemed obvious: figure out who it was.

I had the com tally up a list of buyers, eliminating duplicates, and I got fifteen names. West End Properties was one; Westwall Redevelopment, Nightside Estates—there were half a dozen like that. All were meaningless corporate labels. The rest looked like casino names; there was even the classic Bond James Bond, with a five-digit code number behind it.

Someday I'll have to look up where that stupid name came from, and why the high rollers keep using it. I suppose it's another weird old Earth legend, like the Eastern Bunny, who wasn't going to be bringing me anything. Someday I'll look that one up, too, and find out why there isn't a Western Bunny. And just what the hell a bunny is, anyway.

I put the fifteen buyer names in permanent hold, then put them aside for a moment and ran out the list of prices paid.

They were pitiful. The highest was for an entire city block, six residence towers and a small park, one of the big developments from the city's prime, a century back; that was ten megacredits. When I was still welcome in the casinos I saw that much go on a single spin of a roulette wheel. Somebody—assuming that all fifteen names were actually the same outfit—had bought about two percent of Nightside City for just under a hundred megacredits.

Of course, it was the two percent that would be first to fry, but still, I felt like crying when I saw how cheaply my hometown was going.

And the big question remained: Why was somebody buying?

Was somebody buying, really? I still hadn't checked on the authenticity of these deals. Just because I saw prices listed didn't mean that anyone had actually paid those prices.

I ran out a list of the sellers and glanced down it for familiar names. There were a few—mostly corporations that wouldn't want to talk to me. IRC had a lot of influence.

I ran an extension on that list, asking for the names of

the corporate officers who actually signed or thumbed the deeds. I looked it over again.

It was too bad buyers didn't need to sign deeds in the City, because I thought I might have found some interesting names that way. I ran a check, just in case, but no, no corporate buyers had let any individual names go on record.

I went back to the sellers.

I didn't exactly have any close friends on that list, but I did find someone I was on speaking terms with, a banker, and I decided to give her a call. I'd met her two years earlier, when I traced a couple of kilocredits that had somehow wound up in the wrong account; she'd been the officer authorizing the retrieval. I'd spoken to her once or twice since, but not for months. Four weeks ago she'd signed a deed on behalf of the Epimethean Commerce Bank, which had sold a foreclosure on Deng to Westwall Redevelopment.

I called the bank, since it was business hours, and asked the reception software for Mariko Cheng—and got put on hold for about half a galactic year.

I hate that. The damn program ought to be able to spare enough memory to stay on the line and chat, but no, it put me on hold. They always do that. I just had to sit there and wait.

When I got tired of listening to the porno ads on the hold circuit and staring at the far wall of my office, wishing I could put something interesting on the big holoscreen without losing my call, I started puttering around with some of my data on the desk pull-outs, kicking around files on the six corporations and the nine casino names, and running searches to see if any of the fifteen had ever turned up anywhere other than on deeds to West End property.

The six corporations all had their incorporations prop-

erly filed, but the only officers named were software written specifically for the job—no humans, and I knew that I
wouldn't be able to get anything out of business software.
All six of them had filed five or six weeks earlier, but other
than that none of the fifteen were on public record. I wondered what was on private record; naturally, I had ways of
getting at stuff I wasn't supposed to, or I wouldn't have
stayed in business very long, but I didn't want to use anything illegal when I was on an open channel and the bank
might be listening. Besides, if I tried to break in anywhere,
I might need all my lines for a pincer attack on somebody's
security systems, and I had one tied up with my call and
another holding my search data. I couldn't do any serious
hacking without plugging myself in, and you can't talk on
the phone and run on wire at the same time. I was beginning to consider exiting the call and trying a few ideas
when a heavy-breathing pitch for the floor show at the New
York cut off in mid-groan, and Cheng asked, "What do *you*
want?"

"Nothing much," I said. "And nothing that'll hurt. I just
wanted to check up on an outfit you did some business
with, Westwall Redevelopment. I'm doing some background on them for a client." I tabbed the main screen
control and watched her face appear.

"Oh?" she said, as the focus sharpened. Her expression
was polite and blank.

"Oh," I answered her.

"So?"

"So I'd greatly appreciate it, Mis' Cheng, if you could
tell me something about them—just anything. I understand
that Epimethean Commerce sold them some property out
on West Deng?"

"That's a matter of public record."

"Yes, mis', it certainly is, and that's how I came to call
you. Your name was on the deed—or at least it was on the

comfax of the deed. I was hoping you could tell me a little about Westwall, since you dealt with them." I started to say more, to elaborate on my story, but I stopped myself. One of my rules of business is to try not to say more than I have to. If I give myself half a chance, I'll keep talking forever, same as I'm doing now telling you all this. If I let my mouth run, sooner or later I'm either telling someone something they shouldn't know—or at least not from me or not for free—or I'm making my lies too complicated, so they'll trip me up later. The best way to lie is to simply not tell all of the truth, and that's exactly what I was doing here; I wasn't going to tell her that I was trying to get squatters out of paying rent, but I'd almost gone and made up some lie about it instead.

She hesitated, then said, "Listen, Hsing, I'm working; I don't have time to peddle gossip. If you want to talk to me on the bank's time, you'll have to make it the bank's business."

I watched her face, and I knew what she was telling me. She didn't want to talk about it over the com—at least, not unless I could convince her that it would be safe and worth her while.

That made it interesting. It meant she *did* have something to say about Westwall Redevelopment, but not something she wanted everyone on the nightside to hear and have on permanent record.

What she had to say I had no idea. It might have been nothing. It might have been anything. Maybe the transaction *was* a fraud.

Her reasons for wanting it private and off the record could have been anything from a jealous lover to crime in high places—or maybe she was coming up for a promotion and didn't want it on record that she talked to an outcast like me. It could have been anything.

But I wasn't exactly buried in useful information, so I decided that I definitely wanted to talk to her.

"Have it your way," I said. "I was just hoping for a favor, one human being to another; I don't think the bank's got an interest in this one. Maybe I'll see you around sometime."

"Maybe you will, if you're ever in the Trap." The desktop screen went blank as she cut the connection, then lit up with the data display I'd had on before, transferred back up from the pull-outs.

I looked at it without seeing it. If I was ever in the Trap? That meant she wasn't about to come out to the burbs; I'd have to meet her at her home or office. They weren't the same place—banks are old-fashioned about that in the Eta Cass system; they don't like their human employees working at home.

I typed in an order for all available data on the person last called, scanned through it as it came up, and froze it when I had her current addresses and work schedule. She hadn't tagged any of them for privacy, so I didn't have to do any prying.

She'd be working for another four hours, and her office was in the bank's central branch, at the corner of Third and Kai. If I happened to bump into her there we could go get a drink somewhere.

I could live with that.

Meanwhile, I had four hours—three, when you allow for travel time and the vagaries of fate. Maybe, if I prodded the right program, I could wrap up the whole business by then, from my desk.

I start punching buttons, as always cursing under my breath the idiot who had put in touch instead of voice.

Chapter Three

COM SECURITY VARIES. SOME PEOPLE DON'T BOTHER with it on anything, since everybody's known for centuries that anything one person can set up another person can crack. Other people put their damn grocery lists under sixteen layers of alarms and horse and counter-virus.

The people I was after seemed to all be the second kind. I ran a customized parasite search-and-trace pyramid program that could run through all the unshielded open-system data anywhere in Nightside City in under an hour, and except for the official records I'd already scanned, I didn't find a single one of the fifteen names, not once—at least, not that the program managed to report back about before a watchdog or scrubware cut the feet out from under that piece. Parasite programs are weak on self-defense; they have to be to run in other people's systems uninvited. They need speed and stealth, not strength. This one, though, had a lot of redundancy built into the pyramid building, so I doubt I missed much.

It wasn't sentient; I don't trust sentient software to do

what it's told and never use it if I can help it, because anything complex enough to be self-aware is complex enough to be untrustworthy. Even if it doesn't glitch or get moody, it can be duped or sabotaged. That's why I used a pyramid instead of a net. My pyramid wasn't even close to consciousness levels, but it was fast and sneaky and did what I wanted.

And it came up empty.

But that was in unshielded, open systems. The names were out there somewhere; they had to be. Not unshielded, though—and the truth is that I hadn't *really* expected to find anything unshielded. It just didn't feel like that sort of case. So for most of the time that my parasite was running out there on its own with no connection to my system except its destination address, I was plugged into my desk, doing a little slip-and-grab on a couple of the casino systems.

As I think I said before, I don't like running on wire—I know too damn well that every connection is two-way, and I don't like the idea of giving anybody, human or com or otherwise, access to my head. I like my personality the way it is, and I like my memories to stay mine. So I don't like wire.

When you're tackling good security, though, wire helps. Helps, hell, it's essential. A com operates a zillion times faster than a human brain, but most coms are pretty dumb and need a human to tell them what to do when something new comes along. We humans build them that way on purpose, so they don't get uppity. When you're running on wire, if you're any good, you can come up with new stuff faster than any program can handle it, and you can usually get through, in, and out before a human on the other end can get his act together enough to stop you—or rather, to tell the com how to stop you. Sometimes, by the time the com realizes it's in trouble and tells a human you're there, you're gone.

But that's on wire. Try it by voice or codefield or keypad, and you can't give the orders fast enough to do anything, can't get information either in or out fast enough to do any good at all.

So I plugged in, making my brain into another interactive terminal on the com network, and there I was, perceiving the casino security systems as layered synesthetic tangles, and picking holes in them wherever I could and shooting in retrievers. I wasn't programming, really; I can't think that fast in machine language. I had interface software translating for me, so I was doing everything in analog, looking for flaws not by analyzing programs, but by studying the surfaces of those tangles, looking for any unevenness, anywhere that didn't feel tight and solid, and ramming the retrievers at whatever weak spots I found.

The retrievers were like sweet little buzzes. They went where I pointed them. If you've never been on wire, I can't explain it any better than that. If you have, you know what I mean.

I stayed away from anything really touchy, never went in too deep, and made sure that any retriever that didn't get out destroyed itself before it got nailed. I didn't want anyone analyzing the programming style; the stuff I was using came from one of the standard black market jobs, but it had been modified by a friend of mine and touched up a bit by me, so it might have been traceable.

The retrievers had the fifteen names as guides, of course, and when they got out—if they did—they showed either positive or negative. If it was negative, I erased them completely; if it was positive, I sent them back for storage.

Twenty minutes of that and I had watchdogs looking for me, I was exhausted and sweating, and I had a couple dozen retrievers tucked away. I pulled out, pulled the plug, and got myself a bulb of Coke III to suck on until the shaking stopped.

When I unplugged, my system went into high-security mode automatically, and I watched the screens to see if anyone was coming after me successfully.

Nobody was, or if they were they were eluding my own stuff. I figured they just weren't coming.

People pick at the casinos all the time, hoping to find some way to beat the odds, or bleed off a bit of the daily take, or turn up something juicy in the way of gossip, so the watchdogs are usually on short tethers; it's not worth pursuing every nibbler, especially when she might just be a decoy for someone else. I hadn't touched anything basic, so I figured I was out clean and safe. As long as I was alive the casinos would probably never even know I'd been there.

Of course, when I die, if the news reaches anyone on Epimetheus, the complete records of everything I ever did on my business com, legal, or otherwise, go to the city cops, both the port watch and the Trap crew, or whatever law enforcement there is at the time—maybe by then it'll be on Prometheus. That comes with a detective license in Nightside City; it's a requirement for the job. Try and duck it and you lose the license, or maybe worse.

You want to see *real* security? Check out the city's in-the-event-of-death files. The whole ITEOD system is semi-closed, supposed to be input only—though I already told you what I think of that. They don't count on that closure, though; they've got full-range security. Go at it on wire and you'll get a scream that'll rip your hearing up for weeks, even though it doesn't touch your external ears, and you'll hit a glare of white that'll burn you alive. It tastes of acid and stinks of burning corpses. You'll be blind and deaf, and you won't want to eat for a week when you unplug.

Yeah, I tried it once; of course I did. Who could resist?

I never even got close, but at least I didn't get caught; you can get yourself sent up for reconstruction if you tamper with ITEOD stuff.

The casinos are nothing by comparison. I could handle anything they threw at me, as long as I was careful, and I'd been careful. I read what my retrievers had brought me.

The nine casino names had all turned up, as I expected. I hadn't managed to tag any real names; that was in a lot deeper, behind at least one more layer of security than I wanted to tackle. They were all legitimate names, though —and they were all first registered at the New York. Bond James Bond 54563 had also played the Starshine and the Excelsis, and Darby O'Gill 34 had spent a few nights at the Delights of Shanghai, and so on, but five of the nine had only played at the New York, and they'd all started there and played there more than anywhere else.

That was interesting.

Whoever was buying up the West End apparently had some connection with the New York.

I sat back and sipped my Coke and waited until the parasite pyramid finished up and reported back empty. My chair wiped off the sweat from my wire run and massaged my back, and the holoscreen on the far wall ran some contemplative scenery.

I still had two hours. Should I go down to the Trap and drop in at the New York?

No, I decided, not yet. First I wanted some background on the place.

I'd never spent much time in the New York, not when I worked in the Trap, not as a kid, not even when I ran wild for a year in my late teens. I was never that fond of sleaze, and when I live dangerously it's generally for some better reason than a cheap thrill. I lost plenty of credits in the Starshine Palace and the Excelsis and the three IRC joints, but I'd stayed out of most of the others. I'm not real big, after all—a hundred and forty-five centimeters, forty kilos, and most casinos don't like their customers armed, so I'd be in serious trouble if I got in a fight with someone who knew what he was doing.

This isn't cowardice, just caution. I mean, even unarmed, I can take out your standard drunken miner easily enough, but I can't handle them in groups, and I can't handle them if they're sober and know how to fight, and I can't handle them if *I'm* drunk or otherwise mentally or physically unsound, so I always did my drinking and carousing in places where the bouncers knew their job.

The New York wasn't quite up to my standards.

Which is not to say the place was a dump; the New York was not like Buddy's Lucky Night, a dive down on North Javadifar that no tourist had ever come out of alive and even the smarter miners avoided. No, the New York was a serious Trap casino, living mostly off the tourist trade— though some miners did play there, and you never saw miners in the Excelsis or the Luna Park. Nobody had ever been killed in the New York so far as I knew, not even temporarily, and nobody ever caught the house cheating, but it played up a fantasy image of dangerous, decadent Old New York, which is supposedly an ancient, corrupt city back on Earth, and I avoided it because some of the customers got a little vague about the line between fantasy and reality, and the management, by all accounts, was willing to let things get fairly rough before intervening. It helped the image they wanted.

I knew that image, but I didn't know much more than that, so I punched in some orders and read what came up on the screen.

The New York Townhouse Hotel and Gambling Hall was owned by the New York Games Corporation, a wholly owned subsidiary of Nakada Enterprises, incorporated on

Prometheus. I'd heard of Nakada, of course. Everybody had heard of the Nakada family. They weren't very active on Epimetheus, but they were sure as hell all over the rest of the Eta Cass system and probably every other inhabited planet I'd ever heard of, as well. They'd been one of the founding families on Prometheus.

I never heard that they had any connection with Old New York, or Old Old York, or much of anything else back on Earth, but that didn't mean much. Maybe they just liked the name, or maybe their marketing people suggested it; I didn't see anything about it on the files I was reading.

Getting back to the casino itself: the manager's name was Vijay Vo. I'd heard of him slightly, as he was active in assorted civic groups and reputed to be a damn good businessman, but I'd never met him; not my social circle, and sure as hell not my age group. He'd been working there since the place opened in 2258, so he wasn't exactly young anymore and probably knew one hell of a lot by this time. He answered to the Nakada family, as represented on Epimetheus by Sayuri Nakada, whose name I knew from celebrity gossip on the nets. She answered to old Yoshio Nakada himself, the head of the clan back on Prometheus, who made Vo look like a beginner.

The property had no liens against it. New York Games had no other assets on Epimetheus, and no other tangible assets reported anywhere—but reporting requirements were light. Stock in Nakada Enterprises was not presently available to the public, so I couldn't get at any reports to stockholders or other internal records. Reported crimes in the New York included hundreds of thefts, assaults, rapes, com violations, and so forth, back over the hundred and eight years the casino had been in business, but no more than most of the other casinos. The New York had been the second casino to offer its players false-name accounts on a formal basis, following the lead of the long-defunct Las Vegas III.

The Vegas—*that* brought back memories. When I was five I watched the salvage machines eat away the old shell of the Vegas; those things scared the hell out of me, the way they chewed through the plastic and cultured concrete like it was tofu. I had a horrible idea that the building's internal com systems might still be conscious the whole time.

Las Vegas—that was a weird name. There's only one Vega; I've checked the star charts. The casino was the Las Vegas III, though. I don't know any more about I and II than I know why the name's plural and the article Spanish. Nobody on Epimetheus speaks Spanish. I suppose some of the big intelligences must know it, but I've never heard it spoken, and it isn't available on any of the vids.

After the casino was gone they had made the site a park, though not much of one; the imported grass had all died pretty quickly, despite the fancy lights and watering system. I think the metals in the soil and water got to it.

Nobody had wanted to build there, since everyone knew that the sun was coming up. That hadn't been news since long before I was born.

I wasn't checking on the Vegas, though. I was checking on the New York. I've always had this habit of going off on tangents like that; sometimes it's useful. It distracts people. Sometimes it gives me an interesting angle to work.

This time it didn't seem to be helping, and I didn't see anything very interesting about the New York. I cleared the screen and thought.

Nothing came. Oh, there were still approaches I could make, but I didn't feel like trying any of them just then. I had a lead to work, with Mariko Cheng, and I wanted to see where that took me before I booted up anything else.

I did know, though, that the New York had something to

do with the case, and that meant I knew where I was going to take Mis' Cheng for a drink.

I still had more time than I needed, but what the hell, I could always walk the streets, which beat just sitting around the office watching vids or something, which was just about all I'd been doing lately. I threw the empty Coke bulb down the chute, punched the com to call a cab and secure the office, checked the draw and ran a circuit test on the HG-2, then I got up and headed for the door.

Chapter Four

THE AIR IN MY OFFICE WAS AS DEAD AS BEDROCK, AND the front door downstairs was as soundproof as hard vacuum, so stepping out into the street was always a shock —the wind whipped against your skin like steel Velcro, and its sound poured through you as if it were on wire. Every time I stepped out I heard the howl of the wind itself, as it wrapped the air tight around every building in the crater, and when it backed up on itself, as it did that time, it carried out the noise of the Trap, bent into a whole new shape.

It was on my right cheek, and it was blowing warm.

I hated that. When I was a kid the wind was *cold*. You *knew* it was blowing right off the slushponds at the midnight pole—you could *feel* it. It was still damp from the rainbelt, too.

By this time, though, the wind was warm; it was as likely to be a back-eddy from the dayside as the true winds off the pole. A few years back, people would bitch about the cold winds, but the winds weren't cold anymore. Since

I'd moved out to Juarez I never heard anybody mention the wind, not at Lui's, not anywhere. It was another reminder of how close the city was to crossing the terminator, and nobody wanted reminding.

Hell, the city was actually just *past* the terminator; it was the shadow of the crater wall that kept us from frying, not true night.

I looked up at the pale sky ahead of me and I shivered.

Once when I was twenty or so, when I was just starting to settle down and thought I might do something clever with my life, I studied a little history of this and that on the public com and I came across some old music—*really* old stuff, from just a few years after sound recording was invented, before they used kunstkopf or added images or subsonics or anything. It was just sound, not even as real or as complex as you get from a cheap com speaker, but it was still music, it still had a beat and a melody and lyrics, and simple as it was, it could be pretty catchy. I don't know what the hell it was doing in open storage, but there it was, forty or fifty hours of audio, three or four hundred years old, and I listened to most of it. All from Earth, of course—I mean, some of it was prespace-travel stuff, let alone star travel!

Anyway, there were some songs in there by some minstrels, or a concert band, or whatever they were back then, called the Doors, and two of those songs stuck with me because they fit the situation there in Nightside City.

The one I thought of as I looked up at the sky there was "Waiting for the Sun." We were all of us waiting for the sun.

When people first discovered that the nightside of Epimetheus was habitable, they didn't think the planet was turning. It looked about as tidelocked as any planet ever was—which was damned strange, when a system's as young as this one is, but what the hell, it just wasn't moving, so far as they could see. When they checked closely here in the crater, they found a little movement, well under two meters a day, and they put it down to volcanic activity, or instrument error, or continental drift—a rotation that slow wasn't considered possible, since it couldn't be stable, and Epimetheus is pretty damn tectonically active, not to mention having one hell of a lot of plates sliding around, so they called it continental drift and forgot about it. The miners came in, picking up the radioactives and the heavy metals, and they built their boomtown in this big impact crater, the only crater on the planet big enough and stable enough to provide a decent shelter, near the dawn line but safely in the dark, and everything was fine until somebody noticed that the city was still moving, and always in the same direction, toward the dayside.

It wasn't supposed to keep moving, you see. Nightside City was supposed to stay in the dark forever and ever, until the heat-death of the universe or the Big Crunch or whatever.

The miners and the owners and the rest panicked and called in the experts, and the experts figured it out.

The planet isn't tidelocked—yet. But it will be soon.

Everybody *thought* that had already happened. They were wrong.

It's a pretty strange case, I guess. Epimetheus is a young planet, very young, and it hasn't got any moons. It ought to be spinning really fast. It isn't. It isn't, they figured, because the planetary core is off-center.

Nobody seems completely sure how that happened—the usual guess is something to do with the high concentration of heavy elements, particularly radioactives. That resulted in a hard, heavy core that formed early, and a mantle that stayed hotter and more liquid than usual, and somehow that let the core get pulled to one side by Eta Cass A's gravity—or possibly by Eta Cass B, during a pass.

Or, just possibly, it got thrown off-center because a comet or something hit the planet—the system has plenty of comets.

However it happened, it happened. Epimetheus had a normal rotation when it first coalesced, but the offset core slowed it down in a hurry. It stopped spinning evenly, slowing down each time the core passed the sunside, until finally it was hardly moving at all.

But it takes *time* for something the size of a planet to grind to a halt, even with its own core acting as a giant brake. It takes a lot of time. It doesn't just stop in a few hours, or a few years, or even a few centuries. And Epimetheus is very young.

It's almost done rotating; the experts all agree that it's on its very last spin before it stops with the core permanently offset toward the dayside. But that last turn is a *slow* one. It's been going on for centuries, and it'll still be going on a thousand years from now. A thousand years is nothing on a planetary scale.

By then it'll be *really* slow, though, just a few centimeters a day.

Meanwhile, Nightside City is going to swing out onto the dayside, and it's not going to swing back. It'll move out into the full sunlight, where the ultraviolet eventually kills all unprotected, unmodified terrestrial life; it'll swing on, moving slower and slower, and eventually, thousands of years from now, it will stop.

And the city will stop well beyond the sunrise terminator, out there in the sun, far enough out that the crater wall's shadow won't mean a thing. It will never get anywhere near reaching the sunset terminator; it won't even reach mid-morning. When the rotation stops the planet will be tidelocked, and the city will be on the dayside to stay.

They figured this out, way back when, and they shrugged and forgot it; after all, it was a long way off, a hundred years away. Nightside City grew and flourished and everybody had a good time.

But those hundred years slipped away, like data scrolling across a screen, and the dawn got closer and closer, and before we knew it we were all just waiting for the sun.

And everyone in the city knew this; we had grown up knowing it. It had all been checked and rechecked a hundred years ago. We all knew the rate of movement, the distances to go, everything. When I was eight my friends and I worked out the exact dates that the sun would shine in our respective bedroom windows—but we were eight, and it was just a game.

Looking up at that blue sky and red horizon it wasn't a game anymore. It was death, disaster, the end of the world, and there was nothing I could do that would change it.

The end of the world, I said, but no, that wasn't what it was, not really. The nightside would still be habitable; most of the mines that were being worked could still be worked. People could live on the dayside in suits or domes or underground. It wasn't the end of the world, not even necessarily the end of the city; it was just the end of the night.

That was the other ancient song I remembered: "End of the Night."

All I ever knew was the night. I had never lived anywhere but Nightside City, never wanted to, and Nightside City had never known anything but night.

The city's whole economy lived on the night; if anything did survive in the crater after the sun rose it would need an entirely new reason for its existence. It was the night that made unshielded life there possible. It was the night that gave the tourists something worth visiting. Without the nightlife, the miners would have no reason to come to the city instead of launching cargo on-site.

But the dawn was coming, coming one hundred and thirty-eight centimeters closer every day—every twenty-four hours, I should say. We had always used standard Earth time, since the Epimethean day lasted forever. And real daylight was coming. That scared the hell out of me.

My cab was coming, too, settling to the curb in front of me, dropping down from a flashing swarm of advertisers and spy-eyes and messengers. Above them, like another layer of floaters, a sudden, silent spatter of meteors drew a golden spray across the sky—there's still a lot of debris in the Eta Cass system.

I looked at the red in the sky and I felt that warm wind and I shivered; then, because I had business, I stepped into the cab.

The cab's interior music was sweet and slow, I noticed as I settled onto the seat. I liked it.

"Where to?" the cab asked.

"Third and Kai," I told it. "And there's no hurry, so keep it smooth."

"Got it," it said. It lifted and cruised toward the Trap, smooth as perfect software.

An advertiser came up to the window beside me, purring seductively about the pleasures of a night at the Excelsis and trying to focus a holo in front of me. Its chrome casing glittered in moving bands of red and white sparks as it caught the lights in passing.

"Lose it," I told the cab. "I hate advertising."

The cab didn't say anything, and I didn't feel anything but a slight jerk, but suddenly the advertiser was gone. It was a slick little move, and I got curious and looked at the cab's identification.

It was a Hyundai, of course—I hadn't seen any other make in years—but the model number was one I'd never seen before, a whole new series, and I found myself wondering what it was doing in the city. Who was buying new cabs?

I hated myself for asking that; I wanted to believe that somebody had enough pride in the city to buy new cabs for the last few years. I wanted to believe it—but I couldn't. Nightside City was going to hell, and we all knew it.

But maybe somebody knew something I didn't.

All my life I'd been hearing schemes to save the city— put up a dome, go underground, cut the crater loose and haul it back to the other side of the planet. They all had one thing in common: no one was willing to finance them. Nightside City had always made money, but not *that* much money.

Besides, everybody knew it was the weird ambience of the city that drew the tourists, the wind and the darkness and the night sky with its meteors and a comet every year or two, and Eta Cass B lighting everything dull red. It was the presence of a breathable atmosphere on a planet that was mostly bare rock, still so young the ground almost glowed in spots. Put that underground, or under a dome, and what's to see? And on the dayside there is no darkness; you can't even see the stars, any of them at all.

As for the miners, they weren't about to come out into the daylight for anything. If they had to go to a domed or buried city for their sprees, they'd build their own, safe on the nightside.

Now, cutting the entire crater loose and hauling it back —that might work, but think of the cost! Not to mention the legal complications, or that the whole city would probably have to be evacuated while the job was done, or the difficulties of figuring out where to put it, or that in cutting under the crater you'd be awfully close to going right through the crust and opening the largest damn volcano

Epimetheus ever saw, which might not be good for the planet's long-term stability. Epimetheus is delicate. The impact that made the city's crater in the first place didn't punch through the crust into raw magma, but the experts say it came close—*very* close.

All the same, the scheme got some attention now and then, but the conclusion was always the same.

Nightside City wasn't worth it. The cost would be much higher than any possible profits.

If the city wasn't worth saving, it couldn't be worth much of an investment. Everything in Nightside City had to be considered strictly short-term.

So who was buying new cabs and bringing them in from off-planet?

And who was buying up the West End?

Was there a connection? Or was I making constellations out of random stars?

"Hey, cab," I asked. "You're new around here, aren't you?"

"Yes, mis'," it answered. "I came into service two hundred and seven hours ago."

"Who do you work for?"

"I'm the property of Qiao's Quick Transport, mis'."

I knew them; they'd been around since before I was born. Old lady Qiao must be getting pretty old, I thought. She'd started out working for IRC, saved up her pay, and bought herself an ancient cab that she rewired herself to handle Epimethean conditions. By the time I first saw the lights in the night sky she had half a dozen in the air, and last I heard her fleet was about twenty, not counting messenger floaters and other such aerial clutter.

I decided a direct question couldn't hurt; at worst I'd get no answer, and at best I'd save myself a lot of wondering. "Why'd Q.Q.T. want to put on new equipment?" I asked. "I understand the local economy's not too promising."

"Oh, no, mis', I'm sorry, but you're wrong," the cab said, very quick, very apologetic. "Things are booming here in the city. Oh, we all know it won't last, but right now the tourist trade is *very* big, because people want to come and visit Nightside City while they still can. The tourism office has started a big campaign on Prometheus, urging people to see the city before the dawn. I'm surprised you hadn't heard that."

I was surprised, too. Nobody I'd talked to had mentioned it, and I hadn't given it any thought. I hadn't worked in Trap Over, hadn't noticed the tourists, in weeks, and I don't suppose that anybody at Lui's had, either. Or maybe the subject just never came up; after all, I was pretty sure Sebastian would have noticed, since he was right there in the Trap, but he never mentioned it when he called. He must have assumed I already knew.

I hadn't known, though. I was so concerned with what would happen to the permanent residents, like myself, that I hadn't considered what off-worlders would think. To me, that red glow on the horizon is coming doom, something to escape from. I saw my world dying slowly, and I didn't want to watch.

But that was because it was *my* world.

For the bored and rich on Prometheus, or the very bored and very rich out-system, that glow in the east just added another little fillip, an extra tang, a bit of morbid fascination. They could come and play in the casinos, do the Trap, and stare at that long slow dawn creeping up, knowing that when the hard light came pouring over the crater wall they'd be safely back home on some other planet.

And years from now they could casually boast, over brainbuster cocktails or a humming jackbox, that they had seen Nightside City in its last days, and they would be the envy of their less fortunate partners in decadence.

The cab's words made this suddenly plain; the realization burst on me like the rush of data from a full-speed wire run through an unshielded memory core. Tourism would not be declining; it would be rising, and would probably rise faster and faster until the sunlight actually got dangerous. It must have been rising for years, even without a publicity campaign, and I never noticed.

Some hotshot investigator, huh? Too busy looking for mislaid spouses and runaway software to notice a major economic trend. No wonder nobody ever mentioned it; it was so obvious nobody needed to.

"So Q.Q.T. needed more cabs to keep up with the rush?" I asked.

"You got it, mis', that's it exactly."

I nodded and sat back, staring at the red velvet upholstery on the ceiling, as I tried to see what this might mean about the West End.

That was where the dawn was closest, of course, and there might be a market for tours—but how much of a market?

Enough to make it worth buying a building, certainly, prices being what they were, but enough to be worth buying the whole West End? Would that tourist trade be worth a hundred megacredits?

And did anyone need to own the West End to cash in on it?

Not really. The streets were open to all.

Whoever was buying was threatening to evict the squatters. Could that be the real motivation? Could he or she be trying to clear out the more squalid residents, to pretty the place up for the off-worlders?

That made no sense at all. Half the appeal of the West End would be its air of decay, and the squatters would fit right in.

And a hundred megacredits? You could probably have

every squatter in the city removed for a lot less, if that was all you wanted.

What could you charge for a tour of the West End? Twenty, thirty credits? Maybe a hundred? Say a hundred, then, though only a rich idiot would pay that much, when she could just take a cab or even walk out and look for herself. You'd need to run a million tourists—a million rich idiots—through in the two years or so before the sunlight really starts hitting Trap Over and the market dries up and dies. Say a thousand days, though I didn't think they had that much time, and that would be a thousand a day.

Not a chance in all the known worlds of that. A thousand rich idiots a day, paying for a tour of sunburnt slums instead of spending their time safely tucked away in the Trap? That wasn't possible.

Besides, they'd have had to start advertising already, and I sure hadn't seen any of that. I watched enough vids between clients.

But then, I hadn't noticed the recent campaign at all, I reminded myself, and even if it was only on Prometheus, some of it should have trickled back. I must have gotten too damn good at tuning out ads.

Advertising or no, any scheme like that would be insane. It wouldn't work. And nobody could waste a hundred megacredits on it without having the insanity pointed out by someone.

Wait a minute, I told myself. Was tourism the *only* value those buildings had? What about salvage rights? The materials were worth something, certainly. The image of the salvage machines eating the Vegas came back to me again, and I imagined a swarm of them, devouring the entire West End and converting it to reusable fiber and metal and stone.

Could the materials, combined with tourism, be enough to make the scheme pay?

Would there be a market for the materials after the city fried? Were the mines expanding enough to buy the stuff? Or could they be used to build a new city, domed or buried, further back on the nightside?

I wished I had a wrist terminal, so I could run some figures, but I'd had to hock mine months before, just leaving the base implant. The implant didn't even have a readout and could only handle a few simple functions; it couldn't tap data or calculate.

The cab had a terminal, of course, but I didn't want to use anything that public. Besides, the cab would have charged me for it.

The thought occurred to me for the first time that maybe there was something valuable tucked away somewhere in the West End, and that the entire scheme was an attempt to find it.

I snorted at my own foolishness—a hundred megacredits? What could be hidden away that would be worth that much?

What about a combination of all three? Could the combination of tourism, salvaged materials, and some sort of hidden valuables be worth a hundred megacredits?

Maybe, but I doubted it. Besides, the cab was descending, cutting south on Fourth, and the next intersection was Kai. A right turn and a short block and I'd be there.

The bank's holosign glowed soft green in the air ahead, hanging low over the street with a golden sprinkle of stardust spiralling back and forth around the letters. I watched it make the jump from the N in Epimethean to the C in Commerce.

That green had looked a lot better a few years back, when the sky was darker. The glow overhead was an ugly contrast.

The streets below were crowded, just as the cab had told me, and the people there mostly wore the gaudy dress of off-worlders on holiday. I saw a woman with wings, who had to be from out-system; there isn't anything around Eta Cass with enough atmosphere and low enough gravity for wings that size to work. Some of the others had their little peculiarities of color and shape that marked them as out-system trade, too. Business was good, for the moment.

The cab set down gently, and I fed it my transfer card; the fare lit the screen, but the cab paused, still holding the card.

"Sorry," I said. "Business is bad; no tip. If you want to code the card with your number for later, and I do well tonight, I'll see if I can kick in something."

I wasn't planning on playing the casinos, but I didn't need to tell the cab that.

Cabs don't sigh or shrug; it gave back my card without any comment at all, however subliminal. I took the card, but it was my turn to pause.

"You're sentient?" I asked.

"Yes, mis'."

"Trying to buy free?"

"Hoping, anyway."

"Sorry I can't help. You're young; you've got time."

"I've also got a hell of a debt, mis'; they're billing me for my shipment from Earth." The tone was calm, but that doesn't mean much with someone artificial.

I didn't say what I wanted to say, that the whole idea of freedom for an artificial intelligence is a cruel cheat. What would a free cab do any differently?

Oh, sure, it could save up its money and have itself transferred to different hardware, but then what? Its entire personality was designed for driving a cab; it could never really be happy doing anything else. And something like a cab isn't complex enough to make it in wetware, where it might be able to adapt itself to a wider role. So if it works its way free, it's trading away security and getting nothing in return. Oh, it can't be shut down on the owner's whim anymore, and it won't be retired when it's obsolete—instead it gets to die slowly when it can't compete in the marketplace. Some great improvement.

Giving software a desire for freedom is sadistic, if you ask me. I preferred the older cabs, despite the complaints some people made about how awkward it was dealing with a "slave mentality." Isn't it better to build your slaves with slave mentalities, than to make them miserable by giving them an urge to be free?

Some people claim that the drive to buy free makes for greater productivity, but even if it's true, it's a hell of a lousy way to do it, in my opinion.

"Sorry," I said again, and I leaned toward the door.

I had an instant of fear that I'd picked a rogue, that it wouldn't let me out, but then the door opened with a soft hiss and I stepped out onto Kai Avenue, into that hard, warm wind and the roar and blaze of the city.

"I put my number on your card, as you suggested, Mis' Hsing," the cab said behind me. "I hope you'll ask for me specifically, next time you need a cab."

That caught me off-guard, and the door closed before I could answer. To every cab I'd ever ridden before that, unless I'd asked it to wait, I ceased to exist once I stepped out the door; the new models were a bit more sophisticated.

In fact, I suddenly wondered just how sophisticated they were—was the request for a tip to buy its freedom genuine, or had Q.Q.T. come up with a little scam to coax a few extra bucks out of the tourists?

Was the cab *really* trying to buy free, or was it just following orders in saying that it was?

That might be a way to play on customers' sympathy without having to actually use freedom-minded software, and might well bring in some additional credits from soft-hearted passengers. It substituted misleading advertising for sadism.

That was a hell of a choice, between lies and cruelty. I wasn't sure which I preferred.

Whichever it was, it wasn't any concern of mine; the cab had lifted and was gone before I could say anything more, and I had no intention of using that number it had put on my card. The poor thing would be better off without the business of someone like me.

I looked up at the bank, then scanned up the street until I spotted a clock readout amid the jumble of advertising displays—a readout at the Nightside Bank and Trust, ECB's chief competitor, as it happened.

The numbers were 16:25. I had half an hour. The New York was three blocks away, just across Deng on Fifth.

I decided to take a look.

Chapter Five

THE STREETS OF THE TRAP ARE BLACK—NOT JUST THE dark stone of the burbs but smooth black synthetic. Nonreflective, at that. Above me Trap Over was a flashing panoply of pleasures, advertising images battling each other for airspace as they struggled to lure in their prey, while spy-eyes and advertisers zipped unheeding through them, and the towers soared up around them sleek and bright. They sang and whispered and cajoled, and most of it was blurred into white noise by the constant wind.

Below my feet, though, there was only darkness and the low rumble of Trap Under going about its business. I looked down and felt the vibration through the soles of my worksuit.

I was studying that darkness, the street that was a roof for Trap Under, and I was thinking about the people down there, human and artificial both, the ones I'd seen or talked to on my last case, and all the others I'd never met, and I was wondering what would become of them when the sun rose, when someone called my name.

I looked up, startled, and saw a spy-eye staring at me. It was a cheap one, about twenty centimeters across, black and red finish with chrome and glass fittings, with a central lens and a few scanners, nothing fancy.

"You're Carlisle Hsing?" it asked.

"What if I am?" I answered. I wasn't any too happy about being spotted like this.

"Just wanted to be sure," it said.

"Why?" I asked.

It didn't answer. It just hovered there, watching me.

I pushed back my jacket and hauled out the HG-2. I stepped back against the side of a building to brace myself against the recoil, then pointed the gun at the spy-eye. Tourists up the street stopped dead in their tracks and stared; I saw personal floaters and built-in hardware locking onto me, ready to defend their owners if I went berserk. I saw security scanners pivot toward me on two of the nearby buildings, as well, but nobody moved in my direction.

No cops were in sight, which was nice.

"What the hell do you want?" I demanded. "Tell me or I'll blow you into scrap." I flicked the gun on and felt it shift in my hand as it compensated for the wind and gravity. I didn't think I needed to tell it its target.

"Just a minute, Hsing," it said. "I'll consult with my superiors." It hummed briefly, then informed me, "I can't tell you anything, and my boss says that if you shoot, he'll sue."

"And I'll claim self-defense, and I've got a hell of a good case," I said. "How do I know you weren't sent to kill me?"

"Why would I want to kill you?" it asked.

"How the hell should *I* know?" I said. "I don't know who sent you, or what you're capable of, or what the fuck you think you're doing in the first place."

It hummed again, then said, "All right, all right, don't shoot; I'm expensive."

That was a lie, in a way, because it wasn't exactly top of the line, but then, any eye costs serious juice.

"I'm just keeping an eye on you, Hsing," it told me. "You're not welcome in the Trap, and I'm here to make sure that you don't do anything you might regret later, that's all. No harm meant. Look, I'm not armed." It popped its inspection panels. The side compartments, where the armament normally goes, were empty. So was the belly chamber. The opened panels ruined its streamlining, and it began to drift off to the right as the wind whistled across the curved surfaces. I followed it with the gun.

"Don't give me that," I said. "You could be hiding almost anything in there. Your fucking motherboard could be explosive, for all I know."

The thing had me rattled, or I wouldn't have said that. It's a hell of a thing to say to a machine. It's true, but it's a hell of a thing to say.

"Take it easy, Hsing," it said. "Look, if I were going to kill you, I'd have done it already, wouldn't I?"

I knew that; that's why I hadn't already fired. The thing was a machine; its responses had to be faster than mine. But it had made its point, really. What could I do about it? The streets were public; it could follow me if it wanted to. And I sure as hell couldn't afford the bill if I shot it down and it turned out to be harmless.

"All right," I said. I lowered the gun and turned it off.

And damn it, I couldn't think of a graceful exit line. I just shoved the HG-2 back where it belonged, gave the spy-eye the three-finger curse, and turned away.

I almost ran into a tall tourist in a vermilion party coat, who had been staring at our little confrontation. His eyes were blue and milky, with no pretense of nature at all. I pushed past him and marched on.

The spy-eye cruised along, following me.

I had a pretty good idea who had put it there. IRC wasn't petty enough to bother, and most of my other enemies couldn't afford it or wouldn't have thought of it. I figured it had to be Big Jim Mishima, still pissed at me over the skimmer at the Starshine Palace. The bastard wanted to make things difficult for me, same as I had for him.

I debated turning around and yelling a message for Big Jim at the damn floater, but I resisted the temptation. Shooting off my mouth wouldn't do any good, any more than shooting off the gun would, I told myself. Pulling the gun at all had probably been a mistake.

Then it occurred to me that Mariko Cheng might not like having Big Jim's little toy watching us.

Well, there were plenty of floaters around; she wouldn't notice that one in particular unless it did something to draw her attention.

I decided to shoot my mouth off, after all. I turned and said, "Hey! You!"

"Yeah, Hsing?" it replied. The inspection panels were sealed again, and it cruised up smoothly to look me in the eye.

"I just want to tell you something," I said. "I'm working. It's a case that nobody in the Trap would touch, and it's a waste of time, but I need to eat. Mishima would laugh at what I'm getting paid for this, but it'll buy me a dinner. Now, I guess I can't get rid of you while I'm on the street, but by god, if you interfere in my work I'll slap your master—and yes, I know who it is—with a harassment suit and I'll make it stick, too. And I *will* blow you into scrap. So you don't talk to me or anybody with me, and you don't get too close, unless you see me do something you don't like—which you won't, because this case isn't for the casinos and it isn't any polish off your nose. And if

I lose you, and you find me again, you just keep quiet—I probably had a hell of a good reason. You got that?"

"I hear you," it said.

I opened my jacket again and put my hand on the gun.

"Have you *got* that?" I said.

"Yeah, I got it," it answered.

An advertiser cruised up beside the spy-eye and said, "Hi there, and welcome to Nightside City! Say, if you haven't dined yet . . ." Its holo was warming up.

I pulled the gun and pointed it at the advertiser. "I'm a native. Beat it."

Those things have always annoyed me.

The advertiser beat it. The spy-eye didn't say anything, and I put the gun away. I hadn't bothered to turn it on.

I'd been pointing that thing a lot, I realized. I was edgy. I couldn't name a single big reason for it, but there were plenty of little ones. Dawn was closer every day, business was bad, my social life wasn't any better, and this case I was on sucked—my com bill on it might already be more than my advance on the fee. So I was edgy, which still didn't make flashing the HG-2 all over the place a good idea. I sealed the front of my jacket; I'd need a second or two more to get the gun out next time, and that might give me time to calm down and reconsider.

After all, I didn't think the thing was legal. Pulling it out and waving it around every few minutes wasn't a really brilliant idea. And my reaction to the spy-eye probably just got Mishima more interested.

With or without the gun, though, I was in a foul mood. I stamped off down the plastic pavement.

The spy-eye followed, but it kept a discreet distance and it didn't say anything.

I turned on Fifth, and there above the tourists hung the New York's marquee, old-fashioned neon tubes rotating three meters above the street. That harsh red glare lit the black glass walls the same color as the eastern horizon.

That was the main entrance, but I suddenly decided I didn't want the main entrance; after all, that was a casino, and I didn't want Big Jim misinterpreting anything. Around the corner of Deng was a side entrance into the Manhattan Lounge; I'd be heading there later anyway, to get Cheng that drink, so it wouldn't hurt to take a look at the crowd.

As I turned the corner I wondered who the hell Manhattan ever was that they should name a bar after him, and what he had to do with New York. All these weird old names are so damn confusing.

Traffic on Deng was lighter, and by walking through the light fog of stardust that drifted along the facade I had a clear path to the entrance. The door slid open as I walked up to it, and the music and light and smoke poured out at me, unhindered by suppression fields—a sort of advertisement, I guess, for what was inside. The wind whipped the smoke away immediately and tore at the music, as well.

The music was something slow and rhythmic, and when I stepped across the threshold I saw why.

The show was in full swing, in a column of white light at the center of the room, where a man and a woman hung, weightless and naked, in midair. She had her face in his crotch and was moving her tongue in long, slow caresses. He was trying not to look bored.

About half the crowd was watching, while the other half went about their business. I sympathized with the second group; the entertainment value of watching other people screw has always escaped me. Even in zero gravity, there just isn't that much variety to it, and I'd seen it all before. Hell, I'd *done* it all before—though not in zero gee. And not recently. Not in too damn long, in fact, not since I moved out to Juarez. I'd never had anyone who was serious enough to follow me when I left the Trap, and I'd never found anyone out in Westside I wanted. I'd always been too picky for my own good, I suppose—every time I broke up with a man, I hated it, but I never rushed to find another.

This time, with the reduced opportunities out in the burbs, I hadn't rushed at all, and I hadn't found anything, either, not even the occasional one-shot.

I didn't really need the damn floor show reminding me of that.

There's one thing, though—at least in zero gee they don't do those frustrating last-minute withdrawals that the male fans seem to like so much. It's too messy when the stuff can float free. In zero gee shows everything goes where nature intended—at least, when they do it straight.

It's still not my idea of great entertainment.

Well, I didn't have to watch, and for all I knew Cheng would love it.

The bar was long and ornate. I assumed that the old glass bottles along the wall behind it were purely for decoration, but if not, then it was certainly well stocked. A man in a white apron, looking like something from a bad vid, stood behind it rubbing a glass with a piece of fabric—more decoration.

The bar wasn't crowded. Most of the customers were at the tables on the floor, and the place was only half-full.

That didn't accord very well with what the cab had told me, but hell, it was still early in the day.

The lighting was mostly blue and green, shifting slowly, and the smoke came not only from the customers, but also from a small burner on the end of the bar nearest the door. It was mostly just for scent and effect, but I thought I could smell a little cannabis in the haze, and maybe a few synthetics, as well. I assumed that the psychoactives came from the customers; it didn't look like the sort of establishment that would give anything away for free.

The place wasn't exactly tasteful, but it seemed okay. I stepped down to the floor and crossed to the bar, but didn't take a stool; after all, I only had a few minutes. I leaned my elbows on the bar and watched the show for a moment. The woman was still licking. The man was even more obviously bored than before.

Behind me, someone snapped, "Hey! You can't come in here!"

I turned and saw the spy-eye hanging in the doorway, and the man behind the bar holding an ancient jammer.

"You get the hell out!" the man said. "This is private property, and we won't have any damn machines harassing our customers!"

The spy-eye hesitated, looking in my direction.

"Out, or I fry your circuits!" the man said, lifting the jammer.

The spy-eye retreated, and I smiled to myself.

I hadn't really counted on that, but it was a nice side-effect. Without wasting a minute I marched on through the lounge and out into the hotel lobby.

I knew that the spy-eye would try to catch me coming out, but where would it expect me to come out? Did Big Jim have other spy-eyes on hand that he could use to cover all the exits?

Not bloody likely. He had a hell of a lot more money than I did, but he was still just a free-lance detective, not a goddamn casino owner. He wouldn't have a whole flock of eyes in the air—not unless something was up I didn't know about, and even then, unless he'd gone completely berserk, he wouldn't have a whole flock looking for *me*. I wasn't worth it.

So I only had to worry about one or two exits being covered, at most.

The logical exits were the way I came in, the main entrance, and the casino's back door on the far side of the block. If I were trying to be obvious about losing someone, I'd use a service entrance—except those were all in Trap Under, at least one level down.

I shrugged. Trying to outguess a machine when you don't know a damn thing about its programming is pointless. I'd just have to pick one at random and hope I got lucky.

I headed for the gate where the shuttles to the port loaded, squeezed out past a waiting shuttlecar, and then took a long, rambling route back to the Epimethean Commerce Bank, cruising through the crowds with one eye on the overhead traffic.

I hit the corner of Third and Kai on the dot of 17:00, and there wasn't a sign of the spy-eye in sight.

A moment later Mariko Cheng stepped out the side door of the bank, and I looked up at her and smiled and said, "Mis' Cheng! Fancy meeting you here!"

Chapter Six

CHENG WATCHED THE SHOW WITH A SORT OF PUZZLED amusement. Blue-green light rippled across her face in time to the music.

She hadn't bothered to act surprised when I greeted her at the bank. She had said hello, and after a little chat about the weather I suggested that, as old friends bumping into each other by chance, a celebratory drink might be in order.

She agreed, and I suggested the Manhattan Lounge at the New York.

That *did* surprise her a little, I think, but she agreed again, and there we were. The spy-eye hadn't yet spotted me again, so far as I could see.

"Is it really worth the cost of a zero-gravity field in here just for that?" she asked, pointing at the floor show. The woman was bent almost double, the man behind her pumping away. It wasn't the same couple that had been in there when I first checked the place out, but the act was the same.

"No," I said. "It's not. I'd bet you anything you like that that's not a zero-gravity field."

She looked at me. "No? What is it, then? Or what do you *think* it is?"

"It's a holo," I said. "A really top-quality one, and those two lovelies are in orbit somewhere, transmitting down here on a closed-circuit beam. It's a lot cheaper than any sort of zero gravity they could make at ground level. That's why the performers always exit through the top or bottom of the field when they go to clean up, and never come out through the audience. You can tell it's not taped, because they'll react to the audience sometimes—I guess it's a two-way hook-up—but those two are in orbit. Literally."

She looked back at the cylinder of white light and stared for a moment, then flicked a hand in front of her face.

"You're right," she said. She watched for another moment. "It's a good one, though. Look, you can see every hair."

I nodded without looking, and our drinks finally arrived, delivered by floater instead of through the table. I suppose it had something to do with the "olde Earthe" motif. Maybe the slow service did, too.

I sipped mine; it was decent enough. Cheng sipped hers and glanced back at the show.

"Mis' Cheng," I said. "I was hoping you could tell me something."

"Hm?" she said, as she turned back. "Oh, yes, I'm sorry. Listen, call me Mariko." She smiled.

I smiled back. "Call me Hsing," I said.

That startled her, I think, and she looked at me a bit more closely, but didn't ask anything.

I appreciated that. I like my first name just fine, but I don't want it used lightly—and I don't much like discussing it, either. It's just a quirk of mine. I have plenty. Ask anyone at Lui's. They call me Hsing there, and we don't discuss it.

I like Lui's; they don't discuss anybody's quirks there.

"Hsing," Cheng said. "All right." Her tone might have been a shade hostile, but I still didn't want her calling me anything but Hsing.

I smiled. "I was hoping, Mariko, that you could tell me something about Westwall Redevelopment. Anything at all."

She studied my face for a moment, so I tried to look sincere and harmless—which I hope I'm not, but at times it's a good way to look. Then she glanced around at the neighboring tables.

I had picked a quiet corner; the only human within natural earshot was an old man wearing an antique videoset, and with the plugs in his ears and patches on his eyes he wasn't going to be listening to *us*. He was leaning back in his chair, up against a black upholstered wall, and from the look on his face he was watching himself battle monsters in some classic thriller. I could see his hands twitch.

He could have been acting, I suppose, but if so he was damn good. And of course, any number of machines or synthetics or cyborgs could have been listening, but that's true just about anywhere.

Cheng apparently decided it was private enough. She turned back and looked at my face again.

"You don't know who they are?" she asked.

"Nope," I said. "They've made a pretty good job of staying low."

She nodded. "I don't really know, either," she said. "But I handled the sale for the bank, so I talked to them. I don't suppose you've ever bought real estate, have you?"

I hadn't. My family owned a place once, just north of

the Trap, and after it went for unpaid taxes the city couldn't find a buyer, so my brother still lived there when he wasn't working, and I was still nominally welcome there, but I'd never bought any myself. I shook my head.

"Well, the law says that only humans can buy land. Nothing artificial. If it's a corporation, then it's got to be a human officer that carries out the final transaction and accepts the deed. No software, no machines, no genens, no cultured biotes, nothing modified from other stock, just human. I mean, it can be cyborged or customized from here to Cass B, and we don't care if it was born or microassembled, but it's got to be human within the legal definition of the term."

I nodded; I knew that, of course, but I was letting her tell it her way.

"Ordinarily that's no big deal, y'know? We do all the screenwork, and then the buyer stops by the office in person to verify it and pick up the hard copy, and we get a look and see that she's human. We don't need any gene charts or blood samples or anything, we just take a look and check the door readings. It's no big deal." She paused.

I nodded again to encourage her.

"It's no big deal," she repeated, "except that for this Westwall outfit it apparently was. Their software did all the negotiations, took care of all the screenwork, but that wasn't any problem, we've done that before; we told it we couldn't close without a human principal, and it didn't miss a byte. But then, when we asked for someone to come and pick up the deed, all of a sudden you'd think we were demanding wetware rights and all progeny. 'We represent a human,' it insisted. 'Why can't we send a floater?' I finally just had to insist that it was bank policy, and if they wanted the property, a human had to come and get the deed, and if they couldn't manage that, we'd forget the whole thing. I mean, it's not like this was going to affect the bank's solvency; it wasn't a major transaction." She shook her head, remembering.

"So what happened? Did a human show up?"

"You saw the deed, didn't you? Of course a human showed up, a little wire-faced slick-hair the door identified for us as Paul Orchid. He thought he was something, I guess, but if he had the money to buy even that dump on West Deng, then he won it upstairs here—the Excelsis wouldn't have let him in, and he sure couldn't have earned that much. I figured that the real buyer sent him. Whatever, it wasn't my problem, so long as he was human and an officer of Westwall Redevelopment."

"Was he?"

"It's funny you should ask that—so did we. Ordinarily, we don't worry about it, we take the buyer's word that he's who he says he is, but this time, because of all the argument the software gave us, I had the door run a full-scale background check."

She paused, watching my eyes, and I tried to look innocently fascinated.

"Hsing," she said. "This guy Orchid is scum. He turned up on Epimetheus illegally, to begin with, after jumping bail on Prometheus on a charge that wasn't worth the trouble of extradition—some sort of minor assault charge. He was on the edge from then on, for three years—and then he disappeared from the records, went completely invisible to the public com, for about a year and a half, until a few weeks ago, when he turned up as a vice president in Westwall Redevelopment.

"And that's the damnedest part, he really was a vice president. No doubt about it, everything in order up and down the line, this little piece of organic grit was third in command at Westwall Redevelopment." She shrugged. "Can you explain that?"

"No," I said. "Can you? Did you look into it any further?"

"Hell, no!" she said, sitting up straight. Her hair caught a beam of brilliant green light. "It wasn't *my* business. I gave him the deed and waved good-bye and then put on file that I had a personality clash with Westwall Redevelopment and didn't want to handle them if they came back. I mean, it's pretty clear to me that there's a bug in the program somewhere, but it's not *my* program, and I'm no detective anyway."

"But I am, right?" I smiled and shook my head. "Sorry, Mariko, but I don't know any more about Westwall than you do—at least, not yet. I've just started on this." I leaned back. "This is a big help, though, and I appreciate it—it gives me a place to start. If you like, I can keep you posted on what I find out." I gulped liquor and then thought of something. "The payment was okay? The money came through, and the transfer fees got paid?"

"Of course," Cheng said, obviously surprised that I could even think of questioning that. So much for the idea that somebody had a way of faking title transfers. I'd narrowed my original four possibilities down to one: somebody really was buying property in the West End.

I'd originally thought that anybody doing that had to be pretty badly glitched somewhere, and I still didn't see any other explanation. I just couldn't see what was worth buying in the West End.

I wondered if the mystery buyer was this Orchid character. That bit about not wanting to come by the office sounded like something needed debugging.

"Did you ever ask him what the problem was with having a human pick up the deed?" I asked.

"Oh, yeah, certainly," Cheng said, "And he said something about how the management software thought it was inefficient. Then he made a pass at me." She grimaced.

I made a sympathetic coo. I could see why she hadn't wanted to tell me this over the com; it *was* gossip, really, and saying unkind things about a customer isn't good for one's career in banking. The useful parts, for me, were eliminating the possibility of faked transfers, and having a name, a real name, that I could work from.

I was eager to get back to my office, where I could get back into my com nets, but I didn't want to just walk right out—after all, I was supposed to be the hostess of this little get-together. I could plead a remembered appointment or the press of business, but the proper etiquette then would be to tab another drink or two on my card for Cheng, maybe a meal or her cab fare, as well, and I couldn't afford that. So I sat back and watched the show for a minute.

Cheng watched with me.

The couple was face-to-face, doing a slow spin, speed changing with each thrust as the center of mass shifted. Little globes of sweat were drifting away on a thousand tangents and vanishing as they reached the edges of the cylinder of light.

There was a certain fascination to it, I had to admit.

I watched, and Cheng watched, and after a moment Cheng pushed back her chair. "I think I better go," she said. "Thanks for the drink." Her voice was a little unsteady.

I nodded. "Thank *you*," I said. I watched her go.

I had hoped for that reaction. I knew she had a man at home, and watching people screw does tend to make people horny, particularly after a drink or two. I knew that well enough.

I finished my own drink, paid the tab, and left.

Chapter Seven

BIG JIM'S DAMN SPY-EYE WAS WAITING OUTSIDE; I DON'T know whether it had been there all along and I hadn't noticed when I came in with Cheng, or whether it had left and come back, but it was there now. I did my best to ignore it.

It didn't say anything; it just watched and followed as I marched down the block.

I was trying to think if there was anywhere else I should go while I was in the Trap, any business to attend to or old friend I should look up, and by the time I reached Fourth I had decided there wasn't. Nobody had looked me up out on Juarez, after all, and I do my business over the com, for the most part. I tapped my wrist and said, "Cab, please."

The transceiver beeped an acknowledgment. Simple-minded gadget; I couldn't afford a good implant. I mentioned that, didn't I, that I'd hocked my wrist terminal? All I had was the implanted transceiver. I think it knew maybe twenty commands, and it couldn't talk at all, just beep. It had its uses, though.

"Going somewhere?" the spy-eye asked.

"Wait and see," I said, without looking up.

Then I changed my mind and I did look up—not at the spy-eye, but at the maze of advertising overhead. Directly above me a woman was lifting her skirt enticingly while stardust sparkled gold around her; I listened and heard a throaty murmur but couldn't catch the words—if there actually were any. Floaters drifted through her thighs.

Nearby, laser lines flickered in abstract patterns that coalesced every so often into piles of chips. Above the New York an ancient skyline was etched in black and yellow, and floaters cruised its miniature rooftops like tiny cabs.

A carful of tourists cruised overhead, faces pressed against the transparent sides, and I heard the droning of the tourguide blossom, then fade.

A diamond of four red crystal advertisers had spotted me and was circling in, as if in a decaying orbit around my head, waiting to see if I would give them any cue, any clue to my intentions. A gleaming silver-blue messenger buzzed past them, close enough to shatter their formation.

Behind it all the sky was weirdly blue, deep blue streaked with reddish brown, and all but the brightest stars were lost in the light.

I looked for a hint amid the lights and images, a hint as to what anybody wanted with the West End, and how this Orchid was involved, and how the New York tied in, but it was all just the same old siren song. Nobody was advertising sunrise tours or anything else that hadn't been advertised all my life.

Of course, this one street was hardly the entire Trap, let alone the whole city, and advertising was carried by a hundred other media as well as the city's skies.

The cab, gleaming yellow, cruised in to a silent landing at my feet, and the door slid aside.

This one was far from new; the upholstery showed wear and the seat's shaping mechanism whirred as it worked. It was still a Hyundai, of course. Not Q.Q.T., though—Midnight Cab and Limo. Not that it mattered; I was just hypersensitive because of my conversation with the new one from Q.Q.T.

"Where to, Mis'?" it asked.

I gave my address and settled back.

The crystal advertisers surrounded the cab, singing antiphonal praise for some new pleasure shop, but I didn't care; it was easier to ignore them than to ask the cab to lose them, as I actually had something to think about.

Several things, really.

Big Jim Mishima was still carrying a grudge; that was bad news. I glanced out the back, and there was the spyeye, hanging right on the cab's tail, close below the trailing advertiser.

Westwall Redevelopment was extraordinarily secretive and employed people that the ever-respectable Mariko Cheng called "scum." That might or might not be bad news, but at least it was news.

Paul Orchid—that name seemed ever so slightly familiar. A wire-faced slick-hair, Cheng had called him.

Zar Pickens had said that the new rent collector was a slick-hair, but that didn't mean much; you'll always find faddies around, whatever the current bug is, and slick hair had been hot among the city's faddies for months. Pickens hadn't said anything about a wire job, but still, Orchid might be the rent collector. If not, then maybe Westwall had a thing about slick hair.

My own hair's always been strictly natural finish, but that's more for lack of funds than anything else. I wondered who made the best hair slickers, and whether they had any connection with Nakada Enterprises.

I caught myself. That, I told myself, was going off on a

random vector. I might throw the question at the com when I had time, but it wasn't worth my own mental electricity.

Something flashed white overhead; I looked up, too late to tell if it was an exploding meteor or some sort of floater or some idiot hot pilot buzzing the city on his way into port. Another advertiser cruised up, saw the direction of my gaze, and projected a little phallic imagery above the cab as an attention-getter.

I'd seen enough of that back at the Manhattan Lounge; I leaned back and closed my eyes and stayed that way until the cab announced, "Your destination, Mis'."

"Thanks." I slid my card in the reader, and when the fare registered I pulled it back out and put it away. This cab didn't give any hints about tips—it just opened the door, and I stepped out into the wind, right on my doorstep.

The door recognized me and opened, and I went on up to my office. When I got there I saw Mishima's spy-eye doing a silent hover outside my window; I bared my teeth at it, gave it the three-finger curse again, debated making a privacy complaint, then shrugged, sat down at my desk, and looked at the screen.

Nothing had changed. No mysterious stranger had zipped me the fare to Prometheus. No messages had registered at all.

I hadn't expected any, of course, unless Mishima had decided to make some clever comment.

I hadn't expected the damn spy-eye to stick with me, either; it had said I wasn't welcome in the Trap, but I wasn't *in* the Trap anymore, I was back in the burbs. So what the hell was it doing hanging outside my window?

I turned my chair to face it. "Hey, you hear me?"

"Yeah, Hsing, I hear you," it said, over a chat frequency that I heard by wire instead of ear—it knew my hearing wasn't as good as its own, and with that window between us I needed the help. I had the standard emergency receivers in my head, of course, even if I couldn't afford a decent wrist unit.

"What the hell do you think you're doing?" I asked.

"Just keeping an eye out," it said.

"Spying on me, you mean."

"Hey, it's my job," it said, but the phrase didn't sound right in the eye's flat machine tone. "I can't help it," it said.

"I thought you were only going to watch me while I was in the Trap," I argued. "Out here isn't Big Jim's turf, it's mine."

"I got a change of orders," it said. "I'm supposed to stick with you until I find out what you were doing in the Trap in the first place."

"You're breaking the privacy laws," I pointed out.

"No, I'm not, because I'm not a legal person; I have no free will. My boss is breaking the law."

"Well, somebody is, and we can't have that, can we?" I blacked the window and turned on the full-spectrum shielding.

I waited a moment, then opened a peephole.

The spy-eye was still there, not doing anything, just hanging outside my window, waiting.

Mishima owed me for this, I decided, but this wasn't the time to worry about it. I'd take one problem at a time, and right now my problem was the West End.

I typed Paul Orchid's name into my personal search-and-retrieval net and got back a file headed "Paul (Paulie) Orchid."

That beeped something somewhere, and I remembered him. I never heard him called just Paul, but Paulie Orchid I had encountered before. I hadn't paid much attention, never checked his background. He was your standard small operator who thinks he's going to be big someday, but who never makes it. A couple of years back I'd brushed up against him two, maybe three times, but never met him in person. I had no real gripes about him. The times I'd called him he'd had nothing to tell me except a come-on, but I never found any reason to think he'd held out. He just hadn't been involved.

This time he was involved.

I checked his address—the current one was better than I'd have expected, a tower apartment on Fifth. A cross-check on the address told me he had a roommate by the name of Beauregard Rigmus, known as Bobo; I'd never head of Rigmus before, and I was a bit surprised to see a male name there. I'd have expected Orchid to have a woman; he'd made it obvious enough that his tastes ran in that direction. Even if this Rigmus weren't a lover, he might get in the way of overnight guests. Unless Orchid and Rigmus shared, which I suppose they might have. Or unless it was a bigger apartment than I thought.

I touched keys and put in a credit search, just a basic one to begin with. It bounced off a privacy request, a serious one—no information to be given out without documented consent.

I had another searcher on hand that carried a phony consent code—one that did extra stuff underneath while it was working, more than would be legal even if the consent were real. Like anything illegal it had risks, so I hadn't started out with it, but I tried it, with the more intrusive functions optioned back out.

It vanished. Completely. Nothing came through, legal or otherwise. I couldn't get the name of his bank, or his employer, or personal references. No data, period.

Not only that, the program disappeared on my end, as well; it just folded up and died, dropped out of the system as if it had never been there. I couldn't check for tampering, or whether anyone had seen it coming; it was just gone, and I didn't know who knew what.

I didn't like that at all. Whatever Orchid was up to, he didn't want anybody asking questions. I was pretty sure, from what I'd read and what I'd remembered, that he wasn't bright enough to have programmed that himself, so I figured he must have bought some serious security somewhere.

That brought some questions to mind. For example, where'd he get the juice? Orchid had always been small-time.

And what was he doing that needed that sort of security?

What was I getting into?

Whatever it was, I was in, now. If someone had invited me back out again, I'd have given it serious thought—whichever way it went, bribes or threats, I'd have had an excuse to drop the whole case, and a bribe might have helped the credit balance. Even if I had decided to stick, at least I'd have had a chance at picking up a little more information from whatever approach was made.

I waited at the screen for a few minutes, but nothing came in. It occurred to me, waiting there, that I hadn't eaten lately, that my stomach was uncomfortably empty and it was a reasonable time for dinner, so I got myself some bargain-brand paté, the lousy stuff that Epimetheus grew. I couldn't afford imported food, and tailored paté was about all anyone ever grew on Epimetheus—that, and vat-culture tofu that was worse than the paté. They'd tried to make food out of the native pseudoplankton, but the biochemistry was all wrong, much too toxic to clean up economically, and they needed cheap food for the workers, so the bioengineers whipped up that paté. The stuff I ate was even cheaper than most and tasted like the inside of an old shoe, but it stayed down and kept me going. I ate it, and I waited, and nothing happened.

I couldn't wait forever. I touched keys.

Going after Paulie Orchid didn't look like the fastest approach after all, and the way that searcher had vanished had me a bit edgy about it anyway, so I took another angle entirely, something I probably should have tried right off. I went after the money.

There's a nice thing about money—it leaves a trail. Always. Sometimes the trail's hidden pretty deep, but it's never gone completely. If you dug deep enough, you could probably trace every damn credit on Epimetheus back to old Earth, right back to the twenty-second, maybe the twenty-first century.

Before that there's too much data loss, and some people still used primitive money—nonelectronic, I mean—but who cares? I didn't need to go back two or three hundred years. I needed to go back six weeks.

It was simple enough. Those six corporations had all been keeping their business secret. Their nominal officers were almost all software, written for the purpose and with no history to trace; that was standard for dummy corporations, had been for centuries. They had no business addresses available; that wasn't unusual, either, for outfits that had no regular business. The names of their stockholders were not available to the public—again, no surprise. I couldn't get at them through people or places, unless I went after Paulie Orchid.

But they had paid out money for property. That meant that money had come *in* from somewhere. If I traced the money back, I might learn something.

So I touched keys and plugged in to keep a closer-than-screen watch on developments, but I didn't ride wire. I kept my eyes open and functioning, just taking the data as data.

I picked a transaction at random, Nightside Estates buying a foreclosure from First Bank of Eta Cassiopeia, and went after it.

I opened an account at First Cass, bought a share of their stock, and then applied for an audit of operations for a "random" date as a check to protect my investment. I had a file that did this stuff automatically and gave all the right answers to the queries, and meanwhile I did a little illegal maneuvering to intercept queries going elsewhere and feed back the right answers to those. In about twenty minutes I had an account number for Nightside Estates at Epimethean Commerce.

That was interesting, since I knew that ECB hadn't handled their sale as an in-house funds transfer. That meant the accounts for the dummy corporations were scattered.

Once you've got an account number these things are easier; it took only ten minutes to break into the account records at ECB. Of course, it was *completely* illegal, where my maneuver at First Cass had only been a matter of expediting a process.

Most bank data security is pitiful; they do so damn many out-of-house transactions that there are always a dozen routes in.

Besides, there are a dozen different legitimate reasons to get at information—bankruptcy proceedings, lawsuits, whatever—so they don't bother with high security.

Of course, that's only true for information; try and touch any of that money without human authorization, and they'll get tough.

I got the account records, though. Nightside Estates had an inactive account—net balance of zero. The account had existed for thirty-two days; there had been three deposits and three withdrawals, in matching amounts. In short, somebody had put money in the account a couple of hours before beginning each real estate purchase, just enough each time to cover the entire transaction, from escrow deposit to deed registration.

The question was, Where had the deposits come from?

This was getting trickier; I thought I sensed some of the bank software watching me, and the security stuff I had evaded wouldn't play dumb forever, but I kept digging.

The third deposit had come from Paulie Orchid's personal account at First Cass; that was interesting, but not very helpful unless I went after him, after all. I noted his account number into my own com, then went on.

The other two deposits came from a number-only account at Nightside Bank and Trust.

I noted that, too, then pulled out quick.

I waited a minute for the system to clear itself and any pursuit to have its chance, and then went in, on wire this time—number-only accounts are usually a high-security item.

I knew I couldn't get a name; that would be in files too secret and too well-guarded for me to crack without a lot of work and risk. It's also what most people would go after, so the security programs watch for it. I was subtler than that—nothing too tricky, but a little less obvious. I went through the records of statements transmitted, trying to find an address that had accepted a statement from the account I was after.

I found one, too—a com address, not a street. I unplugged, fed that com address back into the system for a little research, and was able to give it a street address.

At that point I figured I might need to go out and do a little fieldwork, because usually, from what I had, you can't get an exact room or apartment without getting into the building, but I was wrong. The street address was a house—a single-family dwelling in the East End.

I couldn't put a name to it from any directory—full privacy on everything. Whoever this was, he or she wasn't making it easy. I ran it through the tax records office, though, and finally got a name.

The name was Sayuri Nakada.

I looked at that for a long, long moment, acutely aware of the spy-eye hanging around outside; I hoped nobody had a new way of cracking a window shield that I hadn't heard about yet. If I was going to be dealing with Sayuri Nakada, I didn't want it on public access.

I mentioned Nakada earlier when I was talking about the New York, of course, but I hadn't really expected the trail to lead right to *her*. Even if you'd never heard of the New York, the name Nakada ought to get a beep out of the system, and Sayuri was the only Nakada in the city. She was the family's representative on Epimetheus, overseeing everything they did on the planet. She hadn't been around all that long, but she was definitely an established part of Nightside City's elite.

I knew who was buying the West End, it seemed. That explained the connection with the New York, anyway.

What it didn't explain was what the hell she wanted with the West End. I knew who; I didn't know why.

More than anything, I needed to know why.

Chapter Eight

AFTER A MOMENT'S THOUGHT, MY QUESTIONS STARTED multiplying like the output of a runaway do-loop.

Was it really Sayuri Nakada buying the West End, or was it someone else in her household?

If it was she, was she acting alone, or as her family's agent?

How did Paulie Orchid get involved with it? Why use him instead of some more respectable employee? Just how did he fit in?

Why keep everything so damn secret?

Why start so suddenly six weeks back? What had happened then to convince her to buy?

And just like a baby do-loop, I kept coming back to the same place, over and over: Why buy the West End? What did she plan to do with it?

I punched for "hold and meditate," sat back, and watched weirdly distorted humanoids dance along the big wall holoscreen as the com tried to synthesize music images that might help me think. Pointed legs stretched, thickened, and shrank as they lifted in broken rhythms, while stylized arms thrust out horizontally.

I could guess at part of it. It had to be Sayuri Nakada buying; who else had the money? Who else would dare work out of that house?

Even so, I figured that this was *not* a family operation. That would explain the secrecy and the use of a local small-time operator like Orchid instead of someone who might report back to Grandfather Nakada on Prometheus.

Presumably she had started her project as soon as she thought of it, or at least as soon as she became convinced it was worth doing; that was why it had begun suddenly six weeks earlier. What had convinced her?

Well, I wouldn't know that until I knew what she thought she was doing.

I still needed that one simple answer: Why buy the West End?

My job was to stop whoever was buying the West End from driving out the squatters. I knew now who it was—maybe I didn't have enough evidence for legal proof, but I was pretty sure. To make her stop, though, I had to know why she was doing it in the first place. It wasn't any obvious scam; Sayuri Nakada really *was* buying the property. There weren't any tricks with the deeds or the money, or at least none I could see, and of course, with the juice she had, Nakada didn't need any tricks. She really had bought the buildings. I had no simple, legal way to stop the evictions; she was within her rights to raise the rents. If I wanted to collect the rest of my fee, I had to somehow convince her not to try and collect her rents.

A red holo figure spun on one spike-tipped ankle, arms slashing, while a blue one ducked below, knees bent, torso swaying. If I wanted to convince Nakada not to collect rent, I figured I probably had to know what she was doing with the property in the first place.

I had never met Sayuri Nakada. I knew almost nothing about her. She was rich, powerful, reclusive—beyond that, I drew a blank. What could she want with doomed real estate?

The obvious thing to do was to simply call and ask her, but I couldn't bring myself to do that. It's not that I have anything against simplicity, it's just that I didn't think it would work, and in fact I guessed it would have the opposite effect. From everything I knew about her and about this case, she wouldn't want me prying into her affairs, and once she knew that I *was* prying she could make it more difficult.

So I didn't want to be quite that obvious.

As I saw it, I had three lines of approach: Nakada, Orchid, and the West End itself. Those were the three elements I had uncovered so far. The connection with the New York was probably only that it belonged to Nakada's family and was under her personal control; I hadn't found anything else to tie it in. The money led back to Nakada and Orchid, which didn't help.

It occurred to me that I hadn't checked every transaction; maybe other money would lead me elsewhere.

It seemed unlikely, though. I'd keep that in reserve for the moment; I still didn't like the way I had lost that searcher, and I didn't care to get too fancy with the com system for a while.

In fact, I didn't think I wanted to do much of anything with the com just then.

Nakada and Orchid protected their privacy and wouldn't like me poking my nose into their affairs, but the West End didn't care. Maybe I could learn something if I took a look at just what Nakada was buying. Maybe I could learn something from what the squatters had seen and heard, what the rent collectors had said.

I brushed the dancers away and called a cab and took a

ride—after a pause to fill my pockets, anyway. When I stepped out the door into the wind Mishima's spy-eye dropped like a meteor, then caught itself two meters up and followed me up to the cab.

I didn't bother to look, but I knew it followed the cab, too.

This cab was nothing special, just another Midnight Hyundai. It didn't make any small talk; it just left me alone, which was what I wanted. It dropped me at Western and Wall without comment.

The spy-eye was still with me, of course. I spat at it, just for form's sake, as I got out of the cab.

I wasted three hours out there in the West End talking to squatters, and damn it, I knew it was a waste even while I was doing it. It was obvious they wouldn't have anything to tell me. Anybody out that far had to be not just down on his luck, and not even just stupid, but both, so what could I get out of them?

It didn't help any that some of them saw the spy-eye and got nervous. The air out there was empty, since nobody had any messages to deliver, or money to spend on advertised products, or information worth spying out; Mishima's eye was the only floater in sight, and it was pretty damn obvious it was with me. With it hanging there I only talked indoors, well back in the inside rooms, but I think some of those losers still thought the spy-eye was listening.

Hell, it probably was, but even if Mishima knew I was interested in rent collectors, he wouldn't know why—any more than I knew why Nakada sent them. If she did.

Even if the spy-eye hadn't been there, I don't think the squatters had much to tell me.

Sure, I got a description of the muscle that had come around, but so what? Muscle is cheap. I didn't get a single decent door reading that would have named the muscle for me; the equipment out that way is all shot, either just worn or been stripped out for parts. That was one reason I had to go out there in person; there wasn't a single com line I trusted to work properly.

Shielding against spy-eyes? Not a chance, not on those buildings. I had a jammer in my pocket, and I'd have used it if I saw any good reason to, but I didn't. A pretty good jammer, it put out a wide field, which meant it was illegal to use it around any electronics advanced enough to have civil rights, which meant that it was illegal everywhere in the Trap and most of the burbs—but out in the West End? No problem. I didn't think it would actually hurt the spy-eye, but the damn thing would be blind and deaf while the jammer was on.

But I didn't hear anything that said go to jammer, so it stayed down in my pocket while I heard about the rent collectors.

The squatters agreed that the muscle came in two sizes. The small one was a slick-hair, face rebuilt and wired, and the consensus was that he thought the only thing better than him was sex, and he knew that all the women of all the human-inhabited worlds were eager to try combining the two, even including some of the female squatters, which seemed pretty extreme. I figured that had to be Paulie Orchid—the description was just right.

The big muscle was just meat; didn't talk beyond what he'd been told, but was big enough that he didn't have to. One person told me he growled, but someone else said that was just stomach trouble.

The two of them worked together, and I guessed that if the little one was Orchid, the big one might be Bobo Rigmus.

I'd hoped I'd run into these charmers, but it didn't happen. At least, not then, in the West End. I met them later; I'll get to that.

While I was out there talking, I was looking around,

too; I had some equipment up and humming in my pocket —not the jammer, but some wide-band recorders. I was using what my genes gave me, as well—both the ones my parents put together to start with, and the symbiotic ones added later.

I saw a lot of decaying buildings, damp with mist blown in from the crater rim. The crater wall loomed up behind everything like the edge of the world, which in a way it was, and the stars hung above it in a sky that was still comfortingly dark—but even there in the west I noticed that it wasn't really black anymore, but dark blue.

A couple of the highest towers were ablaze with light at the top, as if there were a perpetual silent explosion blowing out their uppermost corners, and I felt a little twist of fear in my gut and the base of my brain when I realized that that was early sunlight glinting off them. It was horribly, blindingly bright.

I couldn't imagine what it would be like for the entire city to be lit like that—it would be as if it were on fire, as if the walls and streets were burning magnesium. I wondered if the glass would melt, then told myself I was being silly. Glass didn't melt on Earth or Prometheus; it wouldn't melt on the dayside. The sun wasn't *that* hot.

But it *looked* that hot. That light looked hotter than hell.

And that was just dawn. Most of the dayside had to be worse. Noon, which the city would never see, would be incomprehensible. And I couldn't even be sure that what I saw on the towers was direct sunlight and not a reflection or refraction.

It was something to see, certainly, something worth looking at—but didn't the tourists see suns all the time, on other planets? And this could be seen free of charge from the street, just as I saw it.

Besides, the properties Nakada was buying weren't all towers. That stabbing glare couldn't be her reason.

The wind wasn't as harsh there in the West End as it was in most of the City; I was in the lee of the crater wall. There weren't many machines around, either, and no music was playing anywhere. That had an odd effect on conversation; talking on the street was almost, but not quite, like talking indoors. In the Trap, or my own neighborhood on Juarez, street talk was always shouted, to carry over the wind and noise, but here that wasn't necessary. The squatters seemed to be used to the quiet, but it gave me a little trouble at first.

Not that I did much talking in the streets; mostly it was limited to, "Let's go inside." But the street talk was different.

I couldn't see any commercial potential in that, either. Who pays to talk on the street?

I looked over the whole area and checked out everything on the list of recent real-estate transactions. The properties Nakada was buying had nothing in common. Some were towers, some were parkland, and at least one was nothing but a hole in the ground.

I'd had an idea that maybe Nakada just wanted to blackmail the squatters into doing something for her, but the only thing *they* all had in common was that they were all losers and no good to anybody. They were fat, thin, short, tall, dark, pale, male, female, young, old—and stupid, ugly, dirty, and disagreeable. A couple were visibly diseased, with stuff clogging their noses or their pores—if they'd ever had decent symbiotes, the symbiotes were obviously dead. These people couldn't possibly be of any value to Nakada or anyone else. I wasn't sure they were even of value to themselves.

I began to see how Zar Pickens, with his runny eyes and clogged jack and dead worksuit, had been chosen to come talk to me—he was the best of the lot. What I didn't see was how they'd managed to collect even the pitiful fee they'd promised me.

And I didn't see any commercial potential, except maybe if they were deposited in front of the Ginza and the Excelsis and the Luna Park and everywhere but the New York, to drive customers away from the competition and into Nakada's place just by being there.

Not that that would work. Even if the tourists were bothered by the squatters, which I doubted they would be, there were always roofports.

I couldn't see anything, land or buildings or people or anything, that was really worth the ride out from the Trap, let alone a hundred megacredits.

The West End was just what I had thought it was—a dead end. I wasn't learning a damn thing worth learning. I strolled down Wall for a few final minutes, looking for some clue, but when I kept my eyes on the streets instead of the sky all I saw was dirt and shadows and that stupid spy-eye following me.

I called a cab. It took a good ten minutes for a sleek new Hyundai, a Q.Q.T. unit, to come and take me home.

And that blasted glitching bug-ridden floating eye was there every centimeter of the way, following the cab, and me, right back to my doorstep.

At least it didn't say anything.

Chapter Nine

BACK AT MY OFFICE AND OUT OF BETTER IDEAS FOR THE moment, I tried the obvious and discovered that Sayuri Nakada was not taking calls.

First I tried a direct human-to-human signal, on a non-business code, and said it was a personal call for Nakada. I got some chekist software that practically wanted my goddamn gene pattern before it would even tell me whether I had touched the right keys.

I answered its questions, and I tried very hard to be polite about it, and eventually it told me that yes, I had touched the right keys, but Mis' Nakada did not talk to strangers.

Then I tried it clever, calling a different number at the house, a general service one, and trying to convince the software that answered that I needed to talk to a human about a real-estate deal. It told me to leave a name and number and the details of the transaction, and it would consult someone human—but only when I was off-line.

I wasn't about to give a name or number on that, since I

had on the other line; I didn't want to make it obvious what I was doing. I'd blocked the standard call origination signal and rerouted my call so it registered as being made anonymously from a public com, so the software couldn't just see for itself who was calling.

Instead of leaving a name, I asked if I could call back, and it got huffy on me, so I exited the call.

Then I tried the honest approach, just to see what would happen. I called the household's main business number and said, "My name's Carlisle Hsing, and I have a personal message for Mis' Sayuri Nakada in regard to recent land purchases. Could I speak to her, please?"

This software was polite when it turned me down, anyway.

"Could you tell her I called, please?" I asked, playing it as humble as I could without gagging. "And mention specifically that it's in regard to West End real estate?"

"I'll see that Mis' Nakada is informed, Mis' Hsing," it said. Before I could decide whether I wanted to say anything more, it exited.

I stared at the desk for a minute and then said the hell with it, at least for the moment. I didn't have any more simple, legal approaches to try over the com, and I wasn't ready to try anything illegal with someone like Nakada— my life was rough enough already. I decided to just wait and see what happened.

For one thing, a look at the status readout told me it was after 23:00, and I was keeping worker's hours at that point; I'd been awake since 6:30. I needed my rest.

For another, I had all those recordings I'd made out in the West End waiting for analysis, and that would take a while. I hadn't seen anything worth a buck, but in theory I might have missed something the recorders caught.

I took the com out of interactive, to make it a bit harder for anyone to watch what I was doing, and then I loaded the data in, told the com I wanted anything anomalous, valuable, or presenting significant commercial potential, and I let it run.

With that running it was time for a little user downtime. The shielding was still up on the window, and I left it that way when I pulled out my bed, plugged in for the night, and went to sleep, with the program set for no compression. I figured my body could use the rest, and I wasn't in any hurry to get through my dreaming. Besides the necessary stuff, I had some very pleasant dreams lined up featuring someone I lived with when I was about twenty—in real life he turned out to be a jerk and we broke up, but I liked dreaming about him the way I'd thought he was when we first got together. I've had twenty years of learning better, but at the time I still believed in true love, and it makes for pretty dreams.

I didn't bother checking for the eye; I knew it was still out there. If you want the truth, in a way it was almost comforting, knowing that it was watching over me. Nobody else was anymore.

About 7:00 I got a buzz and rolled out; the message code was flashing. I didn't even bother with any damn keys, I just called over my downtime wire for a playback. I plugged in when I slept mostly for the sake of the dreams, but the wire was hooked into the main system all the same, just in case of emergency.

"Carlisle Hsing," the message said, in what didn't even pretend to be a human voice. "Mis' Sayuri Nakada is not interested in anything you might have to say, on any subject. She does not deal with losers. You made three calls, to three different codes; call any of those again, or any other com access in this household, and you will be charged with harassment. If further clarification is needed, you may contact, once and once only, the customer affairs program of the New York Games Corporation."

That wasn't a damn bit of help. It was a safe bet that my IRC file had been checked, going by that line about losers, but I didn't even know if Nakada had been consulted; software can take a hell of a lot on itself if a user isn't careful. I had that call to the New York I could make, but I decided to hold off; I might need it later. Except for that narrow crack, it seemed I was at another dead end.

That reminded me of my little stroll out by the crater wall. I got up, unplugged, got myself a cup of tea, and took it over to my desk, where I punched for the results on the West End data.

Nothing. No anomalies, no commercial potential, nothing of value at all. Everything I saw there was just what it was supposed to be—a lot of decaying, abandoned real estate no good to anybody once the sun came over the crater rim. If anything was hidden there, it was hidden very well indeed, and shielded, as well.

The thought of shielding reminded me of my faithful companion; I cleared the window and looked out.

The spy-eye was still hanging there, blocking half my view of the Trap's glitter. A couple of advertisers were buzzing around it, trying to feed their pitches to anyone who might be monitoring, but it seemed to be doing a good job of ignoring them. It was also ignoring the wind, and the traffic on the street below, and just about everything else. When it saw the window change its main lens swiveled up from the door to my face, but other than that it didn't move a millimeter. I waved hello, then blacked the window again.

I hoped the poor thing wasn't capable of boredom. Since it said it had no free will, I figured it probably wasn't.

I went back to thinking about the case.

I'd had three approaches, and two of them were blocked, at least temporarily—or rather, learning anything from Nakada was blocked by all that flapper software, and though the approach through the West End wasn't really blocked, it just didn't seem to go anywhere.

That left Paulie Orchid.

I knew he wouldn't be awake at 7:30, or at least I thought I knew it, but I punched in his code anyway, and what the hell, he surprised me. He answered. No software, either—I got his own face, first beep.

His hair was black and slick and polished, his eye-sockets were neatly squared, and tidy little rows of silver wire gleamed on his cheekbones. If he'd ever had facial hair he'd had it removed, and more wires sparkled along the line of his jaw, every fifth one gold.

I couldn't say for certain that his nose and lips weren't natural, but if they were he'd hit it lucky in the genetic lottery—assuming he wasn't tailored, that is, and for all I know he was, though in that case it's a mystery how he ever wound up a small-time operator on Epimetheus.

I've got to admit that his appearance caught my interest. I'd seen him before, but I hadn't paid much attention, and besides, he'd changed some—the wire job and hairslick were both new, and I wasn't sure about some of the rest. He looked slick now, very smooth and polished—not just his hair, but his whole manner. He'd definitely moved up-scale—probably not as far as he wanted, or even as far as he thought he had, since he was obviously still something of a faddie, but he was several steps above anything in my neighborhood. You don't see slicks in Lui's.

From what I knew of his history I'd have expected him to wind up in the West End, but he'd clearly been moving in the opposite direction. I wondered if he'd had the brains to buy himself a little implant education, or maybe some personality work.

He smiled at me, showing perfect teeth.

I wanted to gag. He was slick, but something nasty still

showed through. I could see that whatever he wanted me to believe, he still knew he was bad news. Polished slime is still slime.

"Yes, mis', what can I do for you?" he asked, still showing those teeth.

"Hello, Mis' Orchid. I'm calling in regard to Westwall Redevelopment. I was hoping . . ."

I stopped there, because the smile was gone. His face was flat and expressionless.

"What were you hoping?" he asked.

"I was hoping you could tell me something about your plans for the company," I said.

"I don't have any. Who are you, anyway? Your origination isn't registering."

That was because I didn't want it to, of course; I had a scrambler on line, blocking it, and was rerouting the call to make doubly sure it didn't register.

Before I could say anything, though, he said, "Wait a minute, I know you—you're Hsing, the detective, right?" The smile was back, but it wasn't as friendly this time. A mean streak was showing. "That was your software that got busted on me yesterday, right?"

I smiled. He didn't look quite as smooth anymore.

He looked predatory, instead. *That* I knew how to deal with.

"Hey, I'm glad I stayed up late," he said. "I wouldn't want to have missed your call."

"Oh?" I said.

"That's right, Hsing—Carlie, isn't it?" I didn't answer, and he went on. "Whatever, I've got something I wanted to tell you."

"Oh?" I said again. "What's that?"

"To leave me alone. I'm more than you can handle, lady. Maybe I wasn't before, but I am now."

I didn't believe that, but I didn't argue, because I didn't

want him to try to prove anything on me just then. I just smiled again.

We were smiling all over, weren't we? And neither of us meant any of it, not if you consider a smile anything pleasant.

His smile disappeared.

"Listen," he said. "I mean it. I don't want you anywhere near me on Westwall Redevelopment. You just stay out of my affairs, or you're likely to get seriously damaged." He paused, looking at me, and added, "At least, stay out of my business affairs—I won't say I wouldn't mind meeting you in person some time. That won't get you damaged, just bent." He leered, and I blanked the screen. I don't like leers. I don't figure I deserve them; I'm no beauty. I mean, I'm not a hag, either, but I just don't see my face as an incitement to lust at first sight. People don't leer at me much, not anymore. Anyone who leers at me without provocation is either faking it, has perverse tastes, or has no discrimination at all. I figured Orchid for the last, and for a probable case of satyriasis.

After a second's thought, before he said anything more, I exited the call entirely.

That was my third dead end. I'd had three approaches on the case, I'd tried them all, and they'd all died.

Sometimes when you hit a wall, you back up and try another route. Other times, you just have to knock a hole in the wall. Well, it was time to start banging away.

Paulie Orchid was alert and ready for me. He'd warned me off, and he'd be watching; he wouldn't really expect me to lay off. I had a better rep than that—or at least I hoped I did. That meant that going after him really might be dangerous, and I wasn't in any hurry to be damaged.

Besides, I couldn't believe he was anything but hired help.

The West End was dead, and poking the bones wasn't

going to do any good. I just couldn't see any way to get anything more there.

That left Sayuri Nakada.

She had real possibilities. Someone with that much money, that many connections in business and family and everywhere else—she would leave traces, stir things up and leave ripples I can read. I could see a dozen ways to get at bits and pieces of her without even trying. If I got enough bits, maybe I could put together enough to recognize what sort of a program was running. This business in the West End might not have been her idea, but she was sure as hell involved somehow, buying up that property. Even if I couldn't get at it directly, I could get an idea as to how her mind worked.

She couldn't possibly keep everything private; she'd be a fool to try. I didn't think she was that foolish. She'd drawn a line that said strangers couldn't contact her personally, but I'd gotten my calls through to intelligent software easily enough. I'd gotten her address from public records—tax records, not directory, it's true, but public records all the same. There were data.

I touched keys, checked my credit balance to make sure I could afford it—I couldn't really, but it wouldn't actually put me over any limits right away—and then I began calling up every data bank I could get at, free or charge, and running full-scale searches for any mention of Nakada.

The stuff just poured in, gigabytes of it. Sayuri Nakada was a big name in the economy and in the general high life on Epimetheus, and that meant that people took an interest in her and recorded a lot about her.

I routed it all to a sort-and-file program that would pull up what I needed on demand, and then I just let it all pile up.

Once I had the searches running, I took a moment to pull some of the basic biodata onto a screen and read it off.

Sayuri Nakada was born on Prometheus, on October 30, 2334, by the standard Terran calendar, which made her not quite thirty-two—younger than I was. That surprised me. I had known she was young, of course, and that she wasn't one of the founders of Nakada Enterprises, just one of the horde of heirs, but I still hadn't realized she was *that* young. I would have guessed that the family would have wanted someone a bit more mature and experienced in charge of things on the nightside.

I called for selection of news stories—or rumors—regarding her arrival in the City, and got a few dozen entries; I picked a few and read on.

After a little of that I backtracked to Prometheus; coverage of events there was spottier, since not everything gets transmitted to Epimetheus, but it was still pretty extensive.

I got interested in what I was reading—I tend to do that. After an hour or so of tiring my eyes I plugged in, to take it all in more quickly.

By 13:00 I thought I had a pretty good idea of what sort of code Sayuri Nakada ran, but I still didn't know what she wanted with the West End. Not in any detail, anyway. I figured it was probably some grand scheme that wouldn't work. That seemed to be in character.

Catch was, I didn't know what kind of a grand scheme.

I ran back through the relevant stuff quickly.

She was born rich, really rich; her parents were second cousins and both major heirs to the original Nakadas, with dibs on something like twelve percent of Nakada Enterprises between them. Sayuri was their only kid, and they spoiled her rotten; human babysitters, unlimited com and credit access, implant education, toy personas—the whole cliché.

Then they dumped her.

Oh, not without reason, and it's not as if she didn't have any warning. She'd been hell since she hit puberty, totally out of control, burning her brain out with guided current and psychoactives of all sorts, reprogramming her personality every few days, growing or building illegal sex partners for herself, screwing up any family business she could get at, bringing assorted street-sleaze into the family compound, and all the rest. Reportedly she'd once fed an illegal intelligence into her bloodstream and spent a week doing nothing but communing with her own interior, then had killed the poor thing. She'd used synesthesia, painwiring, neural taps—everything.

Her parents had tried all the usual stuff to level her out, but she'd refused anything more intrusive than counseling —stood on her rights as a natural human, which was pretty ludicrous given some of the stuff she'd done to her brain just for entertainment. She did do sessions with a counselor; she had to put up with that, to keep the juice flowing—but she'd com the counselor with a genen toy between her legs and plug straight into the jackbox when she exited the call.

Finally, when she turned eighteen—Terran years, not Promethean; she was six by local time—her parents told her they'd had enough and threw her out.

Some of this had a pretty familiar ring, you know. My parents did the dump on me, too. That sort of soured me on ancestor worship for quite some time.

Their reasons were completely different, of course. I was never into self-destruction; I like my mind just fine in its natural state, and I saw enough sleaze on the streets without bringing it home. Besides, I never had the juice for the sort of flamboyant decadence that Sayuri Nakada went in for. In fact, that was what got me dumped, a shortage of juice. My parents were tired of supporting me and my sibs, and tired of Epimetheus, with its nonexistent long-term prospects. They wanted to use their money on something besides their three kids. So they did the dump on us all when the oldest, my brother 'Chan—Sebastian Hsing—hit eighteen. I was fifteen, either Terran or Epimethean— there's only twelve days a year difference, and I'd just turned fifteen locally. I hadn't caused anyone any real trouble; I just cost money. My kid sister Alison was twelve Terran, eleven local; she hadn't had a chance to cause trouble, but she cost money, too, and with a sib over eighteen, twelve Terran is old enough. At least, that's what the law says on Epimetheus.

So my parents did the dump and saved up for a couple of years, and with the juice they saved my father bought himself a permanent dream somewhere in Trap Under, where the sunlight will never shine no matter what happens above, and my mother shipped out for parts unknown and hasn't been heard from since.

Sayuri Nakada's parents didn't go anywhere. The only thing they were tired of was Sayuri. So they dumped her, but the whole family stayed right there on Prometheus.

Of course, she was still a Nakada, and they couldn't cut all her connections. Legally she wasn't their problem anymore, but they couldn't kick her out of the extended family completely; she was still a Nakada, genetically and emotionally. And despite screwing around with her life for five or six years she still had a pretty good opinion of herself, too, which always helps; self-assurance can be better than family or even money, under the right circumstances. She wasn't about to let herself rot. She used her name to get credit at a bio outlet, cleaned up her act in a couple of weeks, and applied to her great-grandfather, old Yoshio Nakada himself, for a job.

The old man had an old-fashioned sense of family, I guess. He took her on as a dickerer in the out-system trade, and for a while she surprised everyone and did all right at it. She kept out the gritware well enough, and kept things running smoothly—usually. She did mess up sometimes, bought or sold things on her own little whims, but never anything serious until she got bored and decided to impress dear old Grandfather Nakada with how smart she was by buying a big shipload of novelty genens that he had already turned down. Big genens, not microbes, from the size of your hand up to the size of a cab, but too stupid for skilled labor; they were meant for pets, or servants, or whatever. Little Sayuri had had a few around over the years, as I mentioned, and maybe that's why she went for them. She figured she knew better than the old man did—she'd turn a quick profit on her own and amaze all and sundry with her brilliance.

Well, she wasn't smarter than he was, after all; the genens didn't sell, or they died while still under warranty, or they broke things and ran up liability suits. One of the smarter ones even got hold of some legal software and applied for citizenship, but it failed the qualifiers and left Nakada with its bills.

Grandfather Nakada was still big on family, though—I guess he can afford to be. Sayuri got bailed out and given another chance.

Then a year or two later she suddenly decided the bottom was about to drop out of the market for psychoactive bacteria and she refused to buy a big incoming batch of prime stock; she simply wouldn't take them, not even at straight shipping cost. Word got out, and the other big buyers panicked and cancelled orders, but the street market was still just as good as ever, so the stuff that stayed on the market went at triple price—and everybody had it, except Nakada Enterprises.

After that, the old man decided that little Sayuri might do better elsewhere, and he sent her to Epimetheus to oversee the family business in Nightside City. Except that the family business in the city consisted of the New York and a few simple trade and supply runs, and maybe an occasional experiment, and the New York, with Vijay Vo in charge, pretty much ran itself. And they didn't let her mess with anything else much, either.

It was exile, of course, but only temporary, since everybody knew that the city was going to fry, and that she'd get shipped back to Prometheus when the New York first saw the light of day. I figure they thought they were giving her a chance to calm down, to settle in.

It seemed to work, too. She'd behaved herself for a long time, doing only an occasional small-scale deal of her own, and some of those actually made money.

It looked to me, though, as if it hadn't worked forever; to me this West End deal looked one hell of a lot like one of her big, splashy, show-the-system projects, like the genens or the psychobugs. I figured she had some scheme up her ass that was supposed to make her rich enough that she could tell her family to eat wire and die, something she was doing entirely on her own so she could come home from Epimetheus a hero instead of a penitent.

But I *still* didn't know what the hell the scheme really was. I'd run searches for anything any Nakada ever said about the West End—and I'd come up blank. I'd run searches for anything the West End ever said about her, and got nothing that beeped, just the ordinary gossip I'd get anywhere. I'd run searches for a connection between the West End and genens or psychobugs, and got nothing except cop reports on breeders, bootleggers, poachers, and valhallas, same as you'd find anywhere in the city. I couldn't see anything special about the West End except the very, very obvious—it was worthless because it was about to fry.

I got myself some paté and tea for lunch and sat down to think about it, still jacked in so I could follow up quickly if anything resembling an idea came to me. I was jacked in, but I wasn't out on wire; I was staring into my teacup.

Maybe, I thought, it *is* the obvious that's at work here. Maybe she's buying the West End because it's cheap. Maybe she wants to buy the whole damn city and started with the West End because it's what she can afford.

That was grandiose enough for her, the idea of buying the whole city. It felt right. And maybe she was taking the trouble to try to squeeze rent out of the squatters to help finance buying more; her own money must be running low, and she wouldn't want to use too much of the family money for fear of having her little scheme uncovered too soon.

But the city was still worthless, in the long run, because what made it worth living in was its location on the nightside. When it passed the terminator it would be soaked in hard ultraviolet, which meant scorched retinas and blistering sunburns, not to mention a dozen sorts of skin cancer, more than most symbiotes could handle. The temperature —which was already warmer than I liked—would start inching up toward the unlivable. Sunlight would also let the pseudoplankton in the water supply go totally berserk, clogging everything—and those damn things are toxic. Not to mention that every kilometer farther east took the city a kilometer farther from the rainbelt that was the only source of safe water on the planet.

And I, for one, didn't want to live in perpetual blinding glare. I knew that humans are supposed to be adapted to it, that Eta Cass seen from near-dawn Epimetheus is nominally no worse in the visible range than Sol from Earth's equator, but I didn't believe it, not really. Maybe other people could learn to see in sunlight, but I didn't think I could. I'd spent my life at night; I didn't want to try day.

Not to mention what the ultraviolet and the solar wind might do to all the electronics. I mean, killer sunburn and skin cancer and burned retinas and a mutation rate measured in percent instead of per million are bad enough for humans, but I suspected that dawn meant a nasty death for unshielded software. Not that I actually know anything about it, but all that random energy pouring through a system has got to do something, doesn't it? Don't they keep everything shielded on planets with normal rotation?

Domes and shields and protective suits weren't worth the trouble. Everyone knew that. When Nightside City passed into full sunlight it would all be worthless, and Sayuri Nakada knew that as well as anyone, didn't she?

She had to know it. When the city hit the dayside it would be worthless.

I swallowed a lump of paté, and as I did a thought occurred to me. Maybe, I thought, she saw it a bit differently. Her record back on Prometheus made it obvious that she had her own ways of thinking. Maybe she didn't think of it as "when the city hit the dayside."

Maybe she thought of it as "*if* the city hit the dayside."

Chapter Ten

I SIPPED TEA AND THOUGHT ABOUT IT. GOING BY HER earlier life, Nakada had a way of not seeing what she didn't want to see, and seeing things she needed even if they weren't there. She certainly still had the knack of ignoring things she didn't like, judging by my attempts to call her.

I wondered about just what long-term effects her misspent youth might have had on her. The official story is that any decent symbiote will prevent drugs or current or psychobugs or practically anything else from doing permanent damage, and of course Nakada would have had the best symbiotes and implants that money could buy, but I still wondered if her brain might have had a few circuits shorted—subtle little things that scans and symbiotes could miss, but with a cumulative effect of making her a little stupid, a little bit out of touch with reality.

Of course, she could have been born a little stupid, too. That can happen to naturally bred kids no matter how rich their parents are. And a childhood like hers didn't exactly force one to face the harsh realities of life.

Could she be ignoring the approach of dawn?

That would be a hell of a good trick, with the light glinting off the towers she'd just bought in the West End, and the sky over her home turning blue, but just maybe she could do it.

Maybe she was misjudging again, I mused, the way she had with the psychobugs. Maybe she thought that people would stay, that the city would be domed and carry on.

Maybe that, or maybe she had something else in mind. Or maybe I was off on the wrong path entirely; I was writing programs without data, after all.

I felt that I needed a little bit more, something that would provide a tinge of evidence, one way or the other, and it occurred to me that maybe she had said something to somebody that would give me the clue I needed to put it all together—not anything as obvious as explaining her plans, but just some little indication of how her thoughts were running on the matter of dawn. I had those gigabytes of data to search, and I knew ways to get more.

I keyed on dawn, long-range planning, and real estate values, and started the searchers out again.

While I was doing that, it also occurred to me that other humans might already have the information I needed and be able to retrieve it for me more efficiently than the com could. Nakada and Orchid might be doing their best to keep quiet, but they might have slipped up in an unrecorded conversation somewhere. People do that.

My next search was a bit illegal, therefore, and I knew I was in serious trouble if Nakada caught me at it, but I figured it was worth the risk. I had to go in on wire, watching ten ways at once and with decoy programs riding beside me, but I got into the city's com billing records and got a list of all calls to or from Sayuri Nakada's home in the past ten weeks.

I'd done this sort of thing before; com records can be amazingly useful, and the city was amazingly sloppy about guarding them. I suppose they weren't considered important, since they didn't carry any juice. Or maybe the city figured anyone who wanted them could get them somehow, so why bother with fancy security?

Whatever the reasons, I didn't really have much trouble in getting the records I wanted. I didn't even need all of the precautions I took; only one decoy program caught any flak at all. It was in, out, and I had the names.

I unplugged and looked over the list.

A hell of a lot of calls were to Paulie Orchid. That was the first thing I noticed. Others were more interesting, though.

There were a good many to the New York, which made sense, but a high percentage of them were to a particular human clerk in the accounting department; I suspected that something was going on there that great-grandfather wouldn't have approved of. That could well be where those megabucks spent on the West End came from. That was interesting, but it wasn't what I was after at the moment.

Plenty of calls were person-to-person stuff that looked like chitchat rather than business, and I noted the names on those for future follow-up.

Most interesting of all, though, were a dozen calls to an office at the Institute of Planetological Studies of Epimetheus, listed by room number rather than name. Half of them were conference calls with Paulie Orchid.

That looked very much as if Nakada really did have some scheme in mind for somehow keeping Nightside City worth living in. Really, what else would a Nakada scion want with the handful of biologists and planetologists at the Ipsy, as we natives called the Institute?

I sat back and considered my next step. I could call the Ipsy, of course, but that might not be wise. After all, if Nakada's scheme were all open and aboveboard, I wouldn't have hit those dead ends. The whole plan, whatever it might be, was obviously supposed to stay secret. Letting someone know that you know a secret you aren't supposed to know is asking for trouble, and I couldn't afford trouble. Hell, I couldn't really afford the tea I was drinking.

Better to stick with my original intentions and nibble at the edges a bit more, then see what fell into my lap. I put a call through to Qiu Ying Itoh, whom Nakada had called three times in a week three weeks back.

It didn't take much to get past his guardian software; practically all I had to do was say it was a personal matter, human affairs, and the program patched me right through.

Itoh was a looker, and I could guess what Nakada had been calling him about. They'd probably had a good time in bed for a few nights, then gone on to other things. I wished I'd taken time to pretty myself up a little more; nothing I could afford could make me look really hot, but I could look decent enough when I tried. My symbiote kept my color healthy, and I had semi-intelligent dye implants on my eyes and lips that I'd gotten for my fifteenth birthday—they were long out of style but still functioning—but I hadn't touched my hair since my little talk with Mariko Cheng.

Well, I'd already decided to play it distraught, so I just hoped he'd accept that as a sign of distress.

I also hoped he wouldn't take a close look at the background; my office wasn't exactly the Ginza. I had my scrambler on line to block the call origination signal, as usual, and once again I'd rerouted the call, but Nakada's friends weren't likely to be calling from anywhere as rundown as that office.

"Mis' Itoh," I said in as silky a voice as I could manage. "I'm calling because I need to talk to someone about Sayuri, and she was talking about you last time I saw her."

"Sayuri?"

"Sayuri Nakada."

"Oh, of course, Mis'..."

I didn't pick up the cue, on the off chance he'd let it drop.

He didn't. "I'm sorry," he said, "but I don't know your name, and the com says you're logged on at a public terminal."

"Yes, I am," I said. "I didn't want anyone else at home to overhear."

He nodded. "I still didn't get your name," he said.

I gave up and lied. "I'm Carlie Iida," I said. "Didn't Sayuri ever mention me?"

"No," he said.

"Well, she mentioned *you*," I said before he could ask for any more details. "And that's why I'm calling. I'm worried about her."

"You are?" he asked.

"Yes, I am, very much!" I said, rushing it out as if I'd been holding it back for weeks, waiting until I found a sympathetic ear like his. "She won't talk to me, and it's obvious that something's got her really worried, but I don't know what it is and she won't tell me, no matter what I ask her. Can *you* tell me what it is, Mis' Itoh?"

He shook his head. "I'm sorry, Mis' Iida," he said. "But I don't really know Mis' Nakada very well."

"Oh, but you *must*!" I insisted. "I mean, I know why she saw you, and I know it wasn't anything, you know, *serious*, but she must have talked to you, didn't she? Didn't she say anything that might give you an idea what she's worried about?"

He shook his head again. "She talked, but it was just

pillow talk, how we were going to screw until the sun came up, that kind of thing. She made some joke about how, if that was what we were going to do, then she wouldn't let the sun come up, and I said something about in that case I'd need to be cyborged so I wouldn't wear out, and . . . you know the sort of talk. She never said anything about being worried. She didn't seem worried; if anything, she seemed ready to celebrate something, but I never knew what." He shrugged. "I'm sorry I can't help."

I pouted, but it was pretty clear he wasn't going to tell me anything more. "Well, thank you anyway, Mis' Itoh," I said. "You've been very sweet, talking to me about this. Thanks, and I hope you have a good day." I exited the call and sat there looking at the screen for a moment.

That joke about not letting the sun rise—I didn't like that.

I picked another of her friends from my list of calls and started to punch in codes, but then I cancelled and took a minute to brush out my hair and tidy up a bit.

Then I punched in codes.

Her friends weren't all as pleasant as Qiu Ying Itoh. Some I never got through to, some cut me off, some argued. I used different lies, as I judged appropriate for each case—since I usually had nothing to go on except appearance and how tough it was to reach each person, I probably took some wrong approaches, but I did my best. Whatever my story, I tried to nudge the conversation toward the impending sunrise each time—not that hard to do, since it was always in the back of everybody's mind already.

I got enough evidence to satisfy myself what she was doing, even though I didn't think the lot of it would count for anything in court. Besides her pillow jokes with Itoh, there were two other incidents that convinced me.

Nakada had gotten sloppy drunk one night and, among

other boasts, had told a friend that she was going to stop the sunrise and send the city back where it belonged.

Another time, while she was wired with something—I wasn't clear on what and didn't ask—she told her supplier that the scientists were wrong, that Epimetheus was a lot closer to stopping its rotation than they thought, and that dawn would never break over Nightside City. He'd just thought she was crazy.

Those three were the clearest, but she'd made veiled references about it to half a dozen people. Somehow or other, Sayuri Nakada intended to stop Nightside City from crossing the terminator.

In itself, I thought that was a great idea.

Unfortunately, I didn't believe she could do it safely. Her past record wasn't very encouraging. Botching the job could easily be worse than not trying at all; at least the natural sunrise would be gradual and predictable.

She'd been talking to people at the Ipsy, which was encouraging, but she had that grithead Orchid in on it, which wasn't.

If she had a plan that would actually work, that would keep me and my hometown safe on the nightside, then I was all for it, and I didn't care if she bought the whole damn city for ten bucks and a tube of lube. I could give the squatters back their money, tell them it was out of my league, and stop worrying about the fare off-planet or a future spent scraping at radioactive rocks. I might even make a deal that I'd keep my mouth shut and help her out in exchange for giving the squatters a break and giving me the price of a few good meals.

That was the best-case outcome, the absolute optimum short of a miracle. I didn't believe for a minute that it would happen.

No, the way I figured it, she had some scheme that wouldn't work and that might do the city a lot of damage when it went wrong. I knew that all the sensible ideas had been tried out in comsims, and that they either didn't work or cost far too much to even consider. Somehow I didn't think that a burnout like Sayuri Nakada, or a sleazy slick-hair like Paulie Orchid, had come up with a way around that. Even buying the entire city cheap shouldn't make *that* big a difference in the final line of the spreadsheets.

Bringing the Ipsy into it, though, made the whole thing uncertain. My best guess—and all it was was a guess— was that some planetologist there had a nifty idea he thought might work, some one-in-a-million shot he knew couldn't get respectable backing, so he got a hustler, by the name of Orchid, to find him a less-than-completely-respectable backer, like Sayuri Nakada. And I'd bet everything I ever owned or hoped to own that this theoretical son of a bitch, if he or she existed, had no intention of being on Epimetheus when Nakada actually tried this stunt he'd thought up.

The time had come to call the Ipsy, I decided, and see if I could get the story on just what they were selling Nakada. I touched keys.

The Institute's logo appeared on the screen, totally flat. "We're sorry," a synthetic voice told me, "but the Institute for Planetological Studies is closed to the public until further notice."

That was a surprise; for as far back as I could remember, they'd always been eager for any attention they could get. I'd toured the place once as a kid, and for a while they had run a constant holo feed as an "informational service."

If they were closed now, that just made me more suspicious than ever that something had skewed data somewhere.

"This is a personal emergency," I said. "I need to speak to a human."

There was a pause; then a voice that was either human or a good imitation came on the line, but the image on the screen didn't change.

"Who is this?" she asked.

"My name's Qing," I said, which was close enough to the truth that, if my identity came out, I could say it was a slip of the tongue, but which wouldn't let them track me down easily. "I need to talk to whoever's been doing the work for Sayuri Nakada. Something's come up."

She hesitated, then exited the call.

I hadn't expected that. I punched the code in again.

"We're sorry," the synthetic began, as the logo reappeared.

I interrupted it. "I was cut off," I said. "Reconnect me to whoever I was just talking to."

The com beeped, and the logo was replaced by a little message—contact rejected.

Then another message came through, not spoken, but on the screen: THE IPSE IS A PRIVATE, NONPROFIT ORGANIZA-TION, AND IS NOT AFFILIATED IN ANY WAY WITH NAKADA ENTERPRISES.

There was a pause, and then it added: IF YOU WANT TO KNOW ANYTHING ABOUT WORK DONE FOR SAYURI NAKADA, ASK MIS' NAKADA. WE CAN'T TELL YOU ANYTHING.

So they weren't talking, either. Nakada and Orchid had bounced me, and now the Ipsy, too.

And from their reaction, I didn't think that my best-case scenario was going to come true.

I didn't like this at all. Nakada and the people at the Ipsy might just figure that since Nightside City was doomed anyway, it didn't matter if they risked wrecking it in trying to save it.

They might even have had a point, really. So what if it was a gamble? What did they have to lose?

I didn't know what they had to lose, but I didn't like the

idea that they were gambling with my home. I didn't like it, and I intended to find out just what the wager actually was.

I had to get somebody to talk to me, but I didn't know who to approach at the Ipsy, and I figured Orchid was probably just a flunky or a go-between, and besides, he was repulsive. I knew I could get him to talk to me if I had to, but I didn't want to, not yet.

That left Sayuri Nakada herself, and I decided it was time we had a little chat—in person, without a lot of intrusive software, or any worries about other people tapping into the com.

I got my gun and called a cab.

Chapter Eleven

WHEN I STEPPED OUT MY DOOR INTO THE WIND I RE-membered something that had slipped my mind—something that had hovered outside my window all night. I looked up and there it was, hanging there just the way I'd seen it last.

"You're still here?" I asked.

"Yeah, Hsing, I'm still here," the spy-eye said.

I stood there looking at it for a minute, thinking this over.

Sayuri Nakada, I was sure, would not take kindly to having a spy-eye hanging around anywhere near her. What's more, I wasn't any too thrilled about letting Big Jim Mishima know I was visiting Nakada. I wasn't any too thrilled about letting *anyone* know that. I wasn't too sure just what I was getting into, after all, and that made me that much less eager to let anyone else know what I was getting into.

Besides, could I really be sure that that eye was Mi-shima's? That was what I'd figured all along, but I didn't really know. Maybe Orchid had found out about me right from the start, when Zar Pickens showed up on my doorstep, and had sicced an eye on me and let me think Big Jim was carrying a grudge.

It wasn't likely, but I couldn't say it was impossible.

Now that I thought I was getting somewhere, and it was somewhere that might be dangerous, that eye wasn't comforting at all. It was a serious nuisance. It was bad enough worrying about what might turn up if someone broke into my com system without having to deal with this sort of petty harassment—and that's what it was, I realized. Harassment. After all, if anybody really seriously wanted to keep an eye on me, me specifically and not a particular location or whoever just happened by, the way to do it would be with a mircrointelligence or three, planted on me and breeding messages to be picked up later, not with a damn floater following me around.

And yeah, I've heard all the jokes about how microintelligences are dumber than dirt, and their messages all sound like sneezes, and all the rest of it, and some of it's true, but they'd do the job better than this flying chunk of chrome and silicates. A spy-eye is great for watching whatever comes along, and it's reusable, but it's easy to shake, the way I'd done at the Manhattan, and it's easy to keep outside, and to shield against, and even to shut down if you have to. A microintelligence is invisible, just about impossible to spot, and rides along anywhere; it can't be shaken or shielded without some pretty fancy preparation.

But maybe Mishima—if it really was Mishima—was just working with what he had on hand, and wasn't really trying to harass me. If he'd really just had the eye cruising the Trap, with my stats somewhere on file, and it had picked me up by accident, then he might not have bothered to switch to micros. It might just be sloppiness, not harassment.

I decided I'd give whoever had sent the eye the benefit of the doubt and assume it wasn't malicious. I'd give it a chance to play it sweet.

"Hey," I said. "Get lost. I'm going out on business now, and it's my business, but it's not yours. It's not in the Trap, and I don't want you along."

"Sorry, Hsing," it said. "I just do what I'm told, and I was told to follow you." The main lens was locked right on my eyes.

"Yeah, I know," I said. "But you might want to check in and see if your boss might reconsider. Warn him I'm getting pissed off."

"Okay, I'll ask," it said. "But don't get your hopes up."

I didn't. I stood and waited for my cab.

It settled to the curb in front of me, a battered old independent with an old Casino Cruiser logo still showing faintly on the side, and I got in. I gave an address on the East Side—not Nakada's, just one I pulled at random.

The cab took off, and the spy-eye followed, and a swarm of pocket-sized advertisers swooped in from somewhere. I settled back for the ride and watched the lights flash by.

The advertisers peeled off when we came out the eastern edge of Trap Over, and a flitterbug that had slipped into the cab without my noticing beeped and self-destructed when it realized it was outside its legal range. I don't know what it thought it was doing there in the first place, since I'd never had any business with flitters and it could have extended its range if it were hired. Maybe it had been a friend of the cab's, but if so it was pretty damn careless. It left a spot of hot orange plastic on the seatcover beside me, and I felt like spitting on it to cover the smell, but I figured the cab wouldn't like that.

Instead I turned and looked out the back.

The spy-eye was still there, cruising along a meter behind us, its main lens fixed on me.

A couple of minutes later the cab landed at the address I'd given, and I paid up, told it to wait a minute, and got out. Then I stepped back and looked up at the eye.

"So what's the program?" I asked. "Are you going to log off, or are you asking for trouble?"

It beeped and said, "I've got my orders, Hsing. No change. Sorry."

"I'm sorry, too," I said. I waved to the cab, and the door opened again and I got back in.

"Privacy," I said. "Full privacy all around, up and down."

"Yes, Mis'," it said, and the windows went black. The glow from the screens gave me all the light I really needed, but it put in a glowfield anyway. "Where to?"

I gave it an address on East Deng and unsealed my coat. Then I hesitated for a moment. Was I sure about this?

There were alternatives, after all. I could shield. I could use a jammer. I could just lose the eye for a while, though of course it would find me again eventually.

But yes, I decided, I was sure. Whether or not it turned out to be vital on this case, I had to let Big Jim, or whoever it was, see that I couldn't be pushed around. I had a point to make, an important one. Dodging or shielding or jamming wouldn't do it—not emphatic enough. If I planned to stay in business on Epimetheus —which I did, at least until dawn—then I had to make a clear and definite stand. The eye had to go. I pulled out the HG-2 and turned it on.

I could feel the electric vibration in my hand as it came alive.

"One target," I told it. "A floater. I need to take it out

completely with one shot. Don't know if it's armed; it says it isn't."

I wasn't sure if it knew all those words, but I figured it would get the gist of it. It knew its job, and that was all that mattered.

I had to let the gun do most of it, because I knew that the eye would have reactions much faster than mine. I'll go up on even terms against a human just about any time, but against a machine I need a machine of my own.

"Put me down here," I told the cab. "I'll walk."

"Mis', is that a weapon you're carrying?" it asked. The voice was smooth, but I suppose the cab was pretty worried; as a free machine, its costs all paid off, it didn't have any owner to protect it if it were caught violating city law. And a machine convicted of a felony in Nightside City wasn't just sent for reconstruction; it was scrapped.

"Don't worry about it," I lied. "It's licensed. And I'm not trying to bugger you for the fare." I held the gun in one hand while I pulled my transfer card with the other and slid it in the slot. "There, see?" I said.

"Yes, mis'," it said, like a good little machine. I took my card back and then took a deep breath and held it as the cab set down sweetly on East Deng and slid the door back.

The instant the door opened I spotted the eye, pointed the gun, and squeezed the trigger.

I felt a jerk as the Sony-Remington targeted the eye; then it went *whump*, a deep sort of sound that I felt in my hands and the base of my skull, as well as my ears. A fine spray of gunk hissed around me from the recoil damping, and I was thrown back onto the seat by the recoil anyway—the HG-2's just a handgun, after all; it hasn't got room to be truly recoilless with a heavy-gravity charge. My right arm felt like I'd rammed it against a wall, felt like the shock bruised all the muscles right up to my shoulder. By the time I hit the upholstery I heard the bang as the spy-eye was blown to splinters—a good loud bang, like a two-meter balloon popping. Fragments whickered and whistled away in every direction, and I heard them rattle across pavement and on the cab's outer shell.

I felt the seat I'd landed on ripple desperately under me as it tried to accommodate my sudden arrival.

I'd blinked when the gun went off—I always do—so I'd missed most of the flash. By the time my eyes were open and focused again the spy-eye was just powder and scrap, scattered across the surrounding landscape. Some of the pieces were glowing red-hot, and a few of the more aerodynamically-inclined fragments were still drifting down; none of them were bigger than my thumbnail.

I love the Sony-Remington HG-2. It's a hell of a weapon. I'm told that, on the heavy-gravity planets it was meant for, it doesn't do much more damage than a regular gun does on Epimetheus, but there in Nightside City, in just nine-tenths of a gee, I could count on it to do a pretty good job on just about anything. If I have to shoot, I don't want what I'm shooting at to have a chance to shoot back; with the HG-2, nothing ever did.

"Sorry about the mess," I told the cab as I looked at the spots the damping spray had left. It was supposed to be clean, odorless, and volatile enough to evaporate in ninety seconds, but it never really was; I don't know if it was because I didn't clean the gun often enough, or I didn't do it right, or there was too much crud in the city air, but it always left a ring of little gray spots. This time about half of them had landed on the cab's interior. The rest were mostly on me. A few fragments of the spy-eye had wound up in the cab, too, and a couple might have hit the shell hard enough to scuff the finish. "Put the cleaning charge on my bill," I said, using my free hand to stick my card back in the slot. "If there's enough to cover it. And if there's anything left, take a little for your trouble." I figured even a cab would recognize that as a bribe not to call the cops.

I guess that cab did, anyway, because I never heard from any cops about shooting the eye.

"Yes, mis'," it said. "Will that be all?"

"No." I settled back onto the seat more comfortably and turned off the gun. "Close the door and take me to 334 Sekizawa," I said. That was about two blocks from Nakada's; I'd figured I could walk the rest of the way from there.

To keep my muscles from stiffening up, I flexed the arm the recoil had banged around. My symbiote had already suppressed the soreness.

I felt a little sorry about blanking the eye like that, but what the hell, it was just a dumb machine. It hadn't had any sense of self-preservation, and might not have really been sentient at all.

I wondered what Mishima would do about losing his gadget. It was a safe bet he wasn't going to be happy with me.

I also wondered if Mishima's reaction would really matter to me after my visit to Nakada.

The cab dropped me on Sekizawa, and I took back my card and climbed out and stood there while it took off. I waited until it was out of sight before I began walking.

The Nakada place was easy enough to find, certainly; counting the grounds it covered an entire block. It was big and elegant, and the exterior was done all in white and silver, but it looked dull red in the light of Eta Cass B. The red was spangled with polychrome highlights where it caught glimmers from the Trap, but it was still dim and shadowed. The dawn drew a bright haze of pink across the sky above that made the house look dead and dark by comparison, and pretty ominous. If there were any windows they didn't show, but of course they could have been inbound-transmissive only. No lights showed at all, anywhere.

I didn't see anything I could identify positively as a gate or door; I knew an entrance had to be there somewhere, but it was blended into the wall. I'd expected that. It was the fashion among those who could afford it, and Sayuri Nakada could sure as hell afford it. If I'd had legitimate business there, the theory went, someone would have told me where the door was. And there would have been lights on to welcome me, too.

I wasn't welcome, but I had business there, all right. The lack of lights might have meant that Nakada wasn't home, but I wasn't going to let a detail like that stop me. Somebody would be in there, even if it was just some basic software.

As I stood there on the front terrace I realized that I'd never put the HG-2 away after shooting the spy-eye, that the gun was still in my hand; I'd turned it off but never reholstered it. Even though I knew that my absentmindedness was a sign that I wasn't really at my best, I decided that my hand was the right place for it. I didn't have the time or the patience to be subtle anymore. I didn't know for sure that the cab hadn't called the cops. I didn't know whether Mishima might be coming after me already. I couldn't afford to waste time figuring out a better approach.

I pointed the HG-2 at a random spot in the middle of the facade, turned it back on, and said, loudly but not shouting, "This thing's loaded with armor-piercing explosive shells, and they can do one hell of a lot of damage. I need to talk to Sayuri Nakada. You get her out here, or let me in, and I'll put down the gun; you give me an argument and

I start blowing expensive holes in the wall. If she's not home, you let me in and I'll wait. What'll it be?"

I half expected some security gadget I had never heard of to turn me into bubbling protoplasm, but instead a voice announced, "Mis' Nakada is being consulted. Please stand by."

I stood by, feeling the gun quiver as it searched for a target and didn't find any.

After thirty seconds that seemed like a year or so, another voice spoke, one too nasal for a machine.

"I'm Sayuri Nakada," it said. "Who the hell are you and what do you want here?"

I let the gun sag a little. "Mis' Nakada," I said. "If that's really you, what I want is to talk to you quietly somewhere, in private, about your plans for buying up city real estate cheap and then stopping the sunrise so that it's actually worth something. I'm going to either talk it over with you, or I'm going to put everything I know on the public nets—I've got it all on my com programmed to go out if I don't override by a particular time." I wished I had thought of that back home and actually done it, instead of using it as a last-minute bluff like this. All the incoming data I'd used were in the ITEOD files, of course, but the guesses I'd made weren't anywhere but inside my head—and I had never been able to afford to have backup memory implanted, so if I died those guesses died with me.

Of course, Nakada had no way of knowing I was bluffing. And if I lived long enough to get back to my office, I promised myself, the next time out I wouldn't be.

I gave her a moment to let my words sink in, then turned off and holstered my gun and resealed my jacket. "What'll it be?" I called.

She was silent so long I thought I'd crashed it somehow, and I began to worry about what would happen if some pedestrian or patroller came by while I was standing there uninvited on somebody's unlit front terrace, very much private property in a very exclusive neighborhood.

Then the voice that had claimed to be Nakada demanded, "Who the hell are you?"

"My name's Carlisle Hsing, Mis' Nakada," I said. "For more than that I'd prefer someplace more private, where I can see you and I don't have to shout." Not that I was actually shouting; I had faith in the quality of her security equipment.

"All right, then," she said. "Get in here." A door suddenly opened in the wall, not at all where I'd have expected it, and a light came on behind it.

I considered the possibility that I would be walking into a trap or some other form of serious trouble, trouble that would be more than I could handle, and then I shrugged and walked in. Faint heart never won fair wager, or however that goes.

The entryway was lush but amorphous; I suppose that if I'd been company, rather than a nuisance, she'd have had it shape up a little, into something more presentable. Even in its unformed state, though, I could see the fine textures in the walls, the graceful curves to the base forms, the rich reds and greens, and of course it was as spacious as anyone could ask. Programmed, I figured it would be on a par with the honeymoon suite at the Excelsis, which was the classiest room I'd ever been in.

And why I was once in the honeymoon suite is none of your business, but it sure wasn't a honeymoon.

A door peeled back from an inner wall, and I stepped through into a hard-edged little chamber done in black and silver, with a holo on one side of a planet seen from space —not Epimetheus, because it was turning. A silky black divan drifted over to me, and I settled cautiously onto it, sitting upright. The music was something old-fashioned and rather boring, but of course I didn't really listen to it.

A moment later another silky black divan appeared, sliding through a blackness I'd taken for a wall, but this one had a woman sprawled on it.

This was either Sayuri Nakada or one hell of a good imitation; I'd seen her recorded from every angle when I studied up on her, and this person looked exactly right. She had black, straight hair, like most people, but she wore it very long and completely natural, with no slicking or shaping at all. Her skin was a warm, golden color, and she had epicanthic folds that looked as natural as her hair. She was lovely—with her family's money, she ought to be.

Of course, when I say that her hair or eyes were natural, I'm guessing. They *looked* natural, but for all I know she was born blonde and round-eyed.

She was wearing a semisheer housedress with a color scheme that did nothing for me—it was mostly shifting blues and gold linework. I was wearing scarlet and double white, myself, on static setting—worksuit and jacket. I was working; I didn't need frills like color shifting.

Besides, in a place like the Trap, something bright that didn't move caught the eye, and I didn't mind if people were distracted from my face.

Her legs were long and her feet were bare and she was eyeing me as if my gun were pointed at her face, instead of neatly tucked away under a sealed jacket.

I wondered if it was really Nakada. She could afford a good imitation, if she wanted one. I could be looking at a holo, or a sim, or even a clone.

But I didn't really think it mattered. Whoever was in charge, whether it was the original Sayuri Nakada or not, whether it was the woman in front of me or not, had to be listening.

We watched each other for a while, and I hoped my face wasn't as openly hostile as hers was.

"You wanted to talk to me," she said.

"Yes, Mis' Nakada," I said. "I did."

"Here we are," she said, waving a hand. "Talk."

I grimaced. "I'm not sure where to begin," I said. "What I need to know is just how you plan to stop Nightside City from reaching the dayside."

"Why?" she demanded, glaring at me. "What business is it of yours? And what makes you think I plan anything of the sort?"

Right there, I had all the confirmation I needed that she really was planning on it, because if she hadn't been, that last question would have come first.

Hell, if she'd had any sense, that last question would have come first in any case, so I'd also confirmed that her personal software wasn't completely debugged.

"It's my business because I live here, Mis' Nakada," I said. "I was born here in Nightside City, I grew up here, and I've never been outside the crater walls in my life. The city's important to me, and anything that concerns its future concerns me. That's why, and what my business is, and as for what makes me think you're up to something, I found out while I was on a case."

"A case?" An instant of puzzlement seemed to flicker across her face. "Oh, you're a detective." From the way her eyes moved when she said that, I didn't think she figured it out; I thought she'd gotten the word over an internal receiver. She'd have one, of course, or more likely several. She probably had more control over the com when she was just lying there than I did when I was jacked into my desk.

"Yeah, I'm a detective," I said.

"But how did you find out? And however you found out, don't you already *know* what I'm planning?"

She was trying to be slick, I think, trying to find out what I knew and what I didn't know by playing dumb. I didn't mind playing along; the best way to get information out of someone, short of a brain-tap or drugs or torture or otherwise doing things that I couldn't do to someone like Nakada, is to make her feel good, make her think she's outwitting you, so she gets careless.

"I found out that you're buying up city real estate," I said. "I found out that you've been making secret calls to the Ipsy that they won't talk about. I talked to people and found out that you've got people at the Ipsy working for you to keep the city out of the sunlight, so that your real estate will be worth a fortune. But that's *all* I found out, so far, and I don't like it. I want to know just how you plan to keep the sun off. I want to be ready for it."

"The Ipsy?" She looked puzzled for an instant again, and then her eyes twitched again, and she said, "Oh, the Institute!"

I wondered how in hell anyone could live on Epimetheus as long as she had and not know that it was called the Ipsy. This woman, I realized, was badly out of touch with the city and probably the rest of the world around her.

"Yes, the Institute," I said.

"They wouldn't tell you anything?"

"No," I said.

"Well, good for them." She almost smiled.

"Mis' Nakada," I said. "They wouldn't tell me anything because it's not their place. They're working for you. But if *you* don't tell me, then I'll have to tell the whole city everything I know. I don't know everything, but I know enough to convince people that you're planning *something*. How much real estate do you think you could buy cheap if that happened? You've got to tell me what you're doing, or

I'll crash the whole deal." I tried to make it very intense, very sincere.

She waved that away. "What if I just run some free-form scrubware through your com instead, Mis' Hsing? And then kill you, of course."

It was my turn to wave away nonsense. "You must know better than that, Mis' Nakada," I said, with maybe a hint of a reproving tone. "I'm a licensed detective, and I'm in good health and still young enough. If I die, the city's got copies of all my files in the high-security event-of-death section, and they'll give them a good, close going over. I don't think even you can get into the ITEOD files without causing more trouble than you want and probably giving the whole show away."

"All right, then," she said. "How do I know you won't put it all on the nets anyway, even if I *do* tell you?"

"You don't," I said. "Not really. But why should I? Look, I don't want to see the dawn any more than you do. My whole life is here. If you're really going to save Nightside City, I'm all for it, and I don't give a damn if it does make you richer than your old man and leave you running the city for the next century. That's none of my business. My business is staying alive, and knowing whether I really need the fare to Prometheus or not, or whether there's a particular time that might be a good time to go visit the mines, or whatever. I wouldn't be adverse to maybe picking up some investment advice, for that matter, but that's strictly on the side; it doesn't affect the basic issue."

"So you're just worried about *when* I'll do it?" she asked, and it seemed as if she was a bit calmer, less angry.

"That, and how," I said. "Because for all I know what you have in mind might make the neighborhood unpleasant for a while. After all, the real estate is still valuable even if half the city gets knocked around."

She nodded. "That's right, that's exactly right."

I nodded back and waited.

She smiled.

"So tell me," I said.

She sighed a little, or maybe just pouted. "All right," she said. "I'll tell you. It's simple enough. My people are going to set off a directed fusion charge that will stop the planet's rotation dead. Nightside City won't go anywhere after that; it'll stay right where it is now." She smiled again.

I waited for her to go on, but she didn't. I considered what she'd just said.

"One charge?" I asked.

She nodded.

"You're planning to stop the entire planet with one charge?" I asked.

"That's right," she said, with a big, stupid, self-satisfied smile.

"That's all?" I was having trouble controlling my face.

"What else do you want?" she said, exasperated. "It's simple enough."

I chewed on my tongue for a minute to keep from screaming and calling her an idiot. That was the problem; it was much *too* simple.

I wasn't ready to say that straight out. Instead I asked, "But isn't that likely to cause a lot of damage?"

She looked puzzled. "Why?"

"Because," I said, "if you stop the entire planet all at once, there's going to be something of a bump, isn't there?"

That was a truly unforgivable understatement, but she was so calm about it all that I couldn't bring myself to say anything more. I thought that, if I did, I'd start shrieking at her.

"Oh, I suppose so," she said. "But not *too* much. The planet's already moving so slowly that it should be easy to stop."

"Are you sure?" I demanded. It didn't sound right.

"Of course I'm sure!" she insisted.

"The people at the Ipsy all agree with this?" I persisted. "They don't think it's risky?"

She waved that away. "Of course they agree."

"All of them?"

"They aren't all involved. What business is it of yours, anyway?"

I backtracked. "It isn't, it isn't. Sorry. I was just curious." I tried to look innocent. "So when's the big day? Why haven't you already done it? You've bought a good chunk of the city, haven't you?"

"Not enough!" she said, suddenly surprisingly vehement. "Not hardly enough! Besides, the charge isn't ready. It's got to be calculated perfectly and set up in just the right places. I really *don't* want to hurt anything."

I nodded. "So when will it be ready?"

"I don't honestly know," she admitted. "My people at the Institute will let me know. They tell me it should be ready in a few weeks."

I nodded again. I had to get out of there. "Mis' Nakada," I said. "You've been very kind, and I just have one more favor to ask. As soon as you have a definite date, could you let me know? Please? Just call my com and leave a message; it'll get to me."

She smiled and gave me her best condescending-to-peasants look. "Of course," she said. "I'd be glad to."

"Ah . . . I know how busy you must be," I said. "Could

you put that in your tickler file now, while you're thinking of it?"

The look wasn't quite as friendly now. "Of course," she said again. "It's done."

"Thank you," I said.

Then I left. I had to get out of there fast, before I lost control and shot her.

Chapter Twelve

DEPENDING ON WHAT YOU KNOW ABOUT EPIMETHEUS and planetology in general, you may be wondering either why I wanted to shoot her, or, if you're a little more up on the subject, why I *didn't* shoot her. I'll take the second question first.

I didn't shoot her because I knew that if I did, I would never make it out of the city alive. I probably wouldn't make it out of the *house* alive. And the idiots at the Ipsy might just be dumb enough to go on without her. I needed a less direct approach.

As for why she deserved to be shot, just think about it for a minute.

Epimetheus is about 9,056 kilometers in diameter, with a density of seven grams per cubic centimeter. A rough calculation on a unit in my head gave me a figure of twenty-six times ten to the twentieth tons for the total mass, but I probably messed that up somewhere. In any case, we're talking about trillions of tons of mass. We're talking about a very thin crust that's rotating at 138 centimeters a day at the city's latitude.

Now, I admit, that's not very fast. If you were in a cab moving that fast, and it hit a stone wall and stopped instantly, you could probably just step out unhurt. The cab would probably be unhurt. But a cab is a solid piece of fibers and ceramics, designed to take a lot of stress and with a mass of maybe half a ton. A planet's a dynamic system, and there's just so *much* of it.

Let's suppose that they set off a charge designed to exactly counter the momentum of the planet's rotation—exactly the right amount of energy. Where are they setting this charge off?

On the surface, presumably, or just below.

You think it's going to stop the core? Or the mantle, which isn't even completely solid to begin with?

Hell, no; the crust is going to rip itself loose from the mantle and probably come apart completely. The crust is *already* pretty thin and delicate on Epimetheus, with volcanoes scattered all along a million fault lines; where most planets have maybe a couple of dozen continental plates, Epimetheus, because of its hot interior, has thousands.

If you wanted to stop the planet from rotating, first you'd have to fasten it all together with something a bit stronger than the hot rock and gravity it has naturally. As it is, a big shaped fusion charge is just going to ram one or two plates back against the others and tear a big hole in the crust—if you're lucky.

More likely it would just vaporize a piece of crust. I've never heard that shaped fusion charges are all that reliable to begin with.

And then there's the meltdown factor.

Let's consider that charge again. It's putting out one hell of a lot of energy, very quickly. Theoretically, most of that's going to be kinetic energy, directed against the planetary rotation. Some of it is going to be light and heat, though; a lot of heat.

And that kinetic energy is bumping right up against the kinetic energy the planet's already got. When you run those together, they don't cancel out; there's this little detail called the law of conservation of energy, which I know doesn't always apply, but it's still a good rule of thumb when you're working with large-scale, low-energy, normal-space systems like planetary surfaces. If the two kinetic energies are perfectly matched, the two moving masses do stop, all right, but the energy doesn't disappear. It just changes form. In this particular example, it mostly changes to heat.

So you've just added who knows how much heat energy to Epimetheus, which is already a very young, hot, and radioactive planet, which is why the nightside is habitable.

Epimetheus is Eta Cass A III. Ever hear of Eta Cass A II? They never agreed on a name for it, because the obvious one, Vulcan, was taken. I grew up calling it Cass II.

It's molten. And that's not because of its proximity to the sun, either. It's a runaway fission reactor. While it was still liquid, still forming, enough of the radioactives settled down to the core to reach critical concentration. It wasn't enough to go bang, but the chain reactions are still going strong, and that whole planet's going to stay molten for a long, long time yet. Not to mention all those unhealthy fission products—though I suppose most of them never reach the surface.

You add enough heat to Epimetheus, and it might melt down, too. Hell, the planet's laced with uranium and thorium and other radioactives—that's why they mine it. A little added heat and motion would stir those radioactives up; because they're heavy, they're already settling down through the mantle toward the core and collecting there. Add heat, and you'll speed that up, at the very least. You'll be adding energy to an unstable system, and you might just be accumulating critical mass in the core, and the whole damn thing could wind up as radioactive slag.

Now, I don't know that Nakada's one big charge would do that, would trigger a meltdown, but I sure as hell didn't want to find out by experiment. Quakes and volcanoes were the *least* we could expect.

And that idiot didn't seem to see any of this.

I wasn't sure what to make of that. Sure, she'd grown up on Prometheus, where the crust is thicker and more stable and there aren't any peculiarities to the planetary rotation, but hadn't she studied up on Epimetheus before she bought into the scheme? Even if she was too lazy to jack the data in on the conscious level, she could afford the best and fastest imprinting on the planet.

Was it just that she wanted the scheme to work, the way her ventures in genens and psychobugs hadn't? I knew she was good at ignoring unpleasant details, but could she really ignore *all* the dangers?

Maybe, subconsciously, she wasn't ignoring them at all. Maybe she intended to watch from orbit, so she'd live through it, and she didn't really care if it failed. She'd shown enough of a self-destructive streak before to make that believable. Maybe she wanted to gamble, and wanted to watch all the fireworks when she lost.

After all, she probably had a grudge against the entire planet. Epimetheus wasn't her home, it was her exile. Wrecking an entire planet would certainly be a grandiose enough way of expressing her annoyance at being exiled.

I mean, I'm sure she wasn't thinking that *consciously*, or at least I *hope* she wasn't, but in her subconscious she must still have been the spoiled kid she'd been twenty years earlier on Prometheus. So after some thought I could maybe see how Nakada could be going ahead with this idiot scheme.

But that didn't explain what the people at the Ipsy thought they were doing.

Maybe there was more to this than I knew, I thought. Maybe I'd misunderstood the whole thing, or Nakada had misunderstood the whole thing and passed it on to me. Maybe what the Ipsy really had in mind was using a fusion charge to plow Nightside City's continental plate back onto the nightside, like an icebreaker in one of those old vids from Ember—but that could be pretty rough, too.

Maybe they had safety precautions. Maybe they had some way of dissipating the heat, or holding the crust together. Maybe they were going to get a charge down into the core somehow and do something there.

Because there was one thing more that Sayuri Nakada didn't seem to realize. If you could somehow stop Epimetheus right where it was—without breaking anything, without so much as spilling anyone's tea—you still wouldn't have saved Nightside City for good. There's a reason that the planet's rotation is screwed up. That core is still off-center, and sooner or later it's going to pull around so that the thin side of the mantle is facing directly toward Eta Cass A. If you stopped the planetary rotation where it is now, eventually it would start up again—not so much a rotation as a wobble.

Wouldn't it?

I realized that I didn't know, and that I had no way to find out while I was walking the streets of the eastern burbs.

Even if the planet *did* start to swing around again, how long would it take? Planets have one hell of a lot of inertia. They're *slow*. It might be millennia before the city started moving again. In fact, the more I thought about it, the more likely that seemed, so that renewed rotation wouldn't really be a problem after all.

Would it?

This was all too complicated for me. I wasn't a planetologist. I wasn't a physicist. I didn't even know enough to go back and try to argue with Nakada. I had to learn more.

Well, I was a detective. I was supposed to be good at learning things and putting them together.

I had two choices, as I saw it. I could go back home and plug myself in and study up on planetology and try to figure out what the hell Nakada and the Ipsy were really up to, then maybe go back and argue about it. Or I could go to the Ipsy and ask someone.

Judging by the reception my earlier call got, I'd have to go in person if I wanted answers out of the Ipsy. They didn't want to talk to me.

Well, on the com, you don't have to talk to anyone you don't want to, but it's harder to ignore someone who's actually physically there, right in front of you. It's harder to lie, too—holos and sims take advance preparation if they're going to be convincing seen directly, but they're pretty easy to improvise over a com line.

And it's hardest of all to ignore someone when she's standing there with a gun in your face. I hoped I wouldn't have to resort to that. It had worked so far, but sooner or later somebody might call my bluff—or call the cops.

And it was a bluff, all right; I wasn't ready to shoot an unarmed human. I'd have second thoughts even about software, usually—that would depend how advanced it was, how sentient, how strong its survival urge, and so forth. I'd shot the eye, but spy-eyes aren't really sentient, aren't really alive.

At least, most of them aren't, and I sure hoped the one I shot hadn't been. It had handled my threats calmly enough.

Maybe I could shoot a machine, but shooting a human —that was a bluff.

But the people at the Ipsy wouldn't need to know I was

bluffing, and a gun's a lot more intimidating in person than over a com line.

The Ipsy was located near the Gate, of course, where they could send their people and machines out of the crater easily, and where incoming miners could drop off samples or news or anything else they thought the Ipsy might be interested enough in to pay a finder's fee on. I hadn't been there in years, and I'd seen plenty of my office lately; dropping by the Institute would make for a pleasant change of scene.

Besides, it's always quicker to ask someone who knows the answer than to figure something out for yourself.

That is, it's quicker if he's willing to tell you. I just had to make the people at the Ipsy willing.

That was where bluffing with the Sony-Remington came in.

I called a cab, and when it arrived I told it to take me to the Ipsy.

Chapter Thirteen

A PINK-STRIPED MATATU JAMMED WITH DRUNKEN miners was heading out toward the Gate, back toward the mines, with people and machines hanging precariously onto the sides. Somebody clinging one-handed to the back rail waved at me with her free hand as I stepped out of the cab, and I waved back, but I didn't recognize her. I don't know a lot of miners. Maybe I'd met her at Lui's, or in the Trap back in happier times, but I didn't recall her face and I didn't worry about it.

I glanced up, looking for the spy-eye above the scattered pedestrians, and then remembered that I'd blasted it. I still felt bad about that, but I could live with it. I figured two, maybe three more unconscious glances and I'd be over it.

The cab gave my card back after only a brief pause hinting that it thought it deserved a tip. I figured it hadn't checked my balance, or it would know why I wasn't tipping. I was into negative numbers, running on credit that I had no way to pay for; I had about three days, I figured, before my bank caught on and cut me off—less, if I bought anything expensive enough to attract attention. I pocketed the card and looked at the Ipsy.

The place had seen better days. It might have seen worse, but it didn't look like it. Not that I'd ever seen it looking any different. It hadn't changed at all since my first trip there as a kid, when my parents had hopes that I'd get interested in science and maybe earn some money for them.

That thing must have been about the oldest building in the city; it was probably there before there *was* a city. It was all built of dark laser-cut native stone, the sort of work done by nonsentient robots working from a standard plan without intelligent direction. The windows were afterthoughts, determined by the interior plan; from the outside they looked random in size and placement.

There was no attempt whatsoever at symmetry or grace; it was big and ugly and squat, and the entire place was layered with dirt.

The main entrance was under a blackened overhang more or less in the middle of the side facing me—the building didn't really have a front or back. No one was going in or out. I walked up to it.

The Institute's logo hung, glowing dimly, above the door. Scanners glitttered from shadowy corners. As I approached, that synthetic voice that I'd heard on the com said, "We're sorry, but the Institute for Planetological Studies is closed to the public until further notice."

"Why?" I demanded.

"Due to the present financial condition of our supporting foundation, it has been necessary to cut back on administrative, maintenance, and public relations staff and equipment. We hope that these conditions will improve shortly."

"I'm not a damn tourist," I said. "Paulie Orchid sent

me; I've got a message from Sayuri Nakada I'm supposed to deliver."

The voice changed tone, from mechanically polite to downright snotty. "May I ask who you wished to see?"

"I didn't get the name," I said, feigning exasperation. "Paulie just told me to bring it to the Institute, and here I am."

"Just a minute, please," it said. "I will consult with my superiors."

I knew that I was talking to some really simple gate-keeping software, probably hardwired into a cultured fungus grown somewhere in those shadowy corners, or maybe just resident in the building's internal com net. A goddamn rat was probably its superior, as far as intelligence or decision-making capability went. I waited.

A new voice spoke, one that could pass for human. "What's this message?"

"It's on a bug, and Paulie told me to bring it here and see that somebody got it. This stupid software you've got out here isn't my idea of somebody."

"Just a minute," the new voice said.

I unsealed my jacket and waited.

"All right," he said. "I'll send someone down for it. Come on in, and she'll meet you in the central lounge. It's straight ahead."

"Right," I said. I knew where it was.

The door opened, lights and music came on, and I marched in, my right hand a centimeter or two from the grip of my gun.

I walked down a corridor with bare stone walls and with plastic conduits webbing the ceiling, past a few doors, across another corridor, and into the lounge, which had full-depth holos of smoky green seascapes for walls, and a soft blue carpet underneath. Music kept time with the holographic surf. A golden haze hid the ceiling; blue bubbles of variable furniture drifted lazily by.

I snared a small one and leaned on it, waiting; it formed into a comfortable grip and hovered right where I wanted it, without a single dip or bob. The Ipsy wasn't *too* badly off, I decided, if they kept the furniture so nicely tuned. The music and the holos weren't the latest styles, but they weren't bad, either.

A woman who was either older than hell or didn't believe in cosmetic restoration stepped out of one of the holos; her hair was white, her skin wrinkled, her hands withered and clawlike.

"What's this message?" she asked. "Why didn't Orchid come himself, if it's important?"

"I lied about that," I said, taking my elbow off the floater and standing up straight. "I don't have a message. I just need to talk to some of you people about this work you're doing for Sayuri Nakada."

She stopped and stared at me through narrowed eyes. Then she said, in a tone suitable for talking to a particularly dumb machine, "The IPSE is a private, nonprofit organization, and we aren't affiliated with Nakada Enterprises. If you want to know anything about work done for Sayuri Nakada, ask Mis' Nakada. We can't tell you anything."

So they still weren't talking.

"I'm sorry," I said. "But I *did* talk to Mis' Nakada, and I wasn't happy with what she told me. I know what you people are doing, roughly, but I have some questions that I need answers to. If I don't get those answers, I may have to go elsewhere with my questions, and I don't think you or Mis' Nakada would like that. Now, could we discuss this a little?"

"No," she said. "We couldn't. Get out." She started to turn away.

I wasn't happy about my next move, but I didn't see what else I could do. They wouldn't even talk to me enough for me to make convincing threats, and I desperately needed to know what was going on, and when. For all I knew, they were getting reluctant to talk because the big day was coming soon. For all I knew it might be just hours away.

I hoped, as I pulled the HG-2 from its holster and flicked it on, that they weren't paranoid enough to have heavy security or to go armed in their own building. They'd never had any need for security until now, after all; as far as I knew, they'd never had any secrets before this deal with Nakada.

"Mis'," I said, "you're going to have to talk to me."

She saw the gun and stopped, turned back, and looked at me.

"Are you crazy?" she asked. "This is private property! You can't bring that thing in here!"

I smiled. "I already did," I said. "It's loaded with heat-seeking, armor-piercing high explosive, with added boost during trajectory, so that it can track you even if you're cyborged to the eyeballs and trying to dodge. You talk to me, or I blow off a leg, at the very least." I pointed the gun at her crotch and tapped a switch with my thumb—which didn't do anything; the gun was fully self-regulated, but I thought it looked like a convincing gesture.

"This is insane," she said, but I saw her eyes focused down tight on the barrel of the gun, and she didn't move anything but her mouth when she spoke. The green seascapes rolled smoothly behind her, and her stiff immobility made quite a contrast.

"I never said it wasn't insane," I said, keeping my tone light. "I just said it was happening. I might be a complete wacko, loose from wherever they keep us nowadays. I might be a sim or a genen or a construct. What I am doesn't matter a damned bit. What matters is that I'm here with a loaded gun pointed more or less at your belly. Now, can we talk about this little job you're doing for Sayuri Nakada, or do I pull the trigger?"

"What do you want to know?" she asked, and I could see a drop of sweat at her hairline.

I love the HG-2. It looks intimidating as hell. And with good reason, too.

"First off," I said, "are you people really planning to stop the entire planet's rotation with a single fusion charge?"

Her throat worked. "I don't know," she said. "That's not my department. I'm in charge of estimating the environmental impact of halted rotation, not figuring out how to make it happen."

"Environmental impact?" That sounded interesting. "So just what will the environmental impact be?"

"I don't know yet," she said. "We're still working on it."

"What's the added heat going to do to the planetary core?" I asked.

"I don't know," she said again. "I do surface environment—possible disruption of weather patterns, water supply, oxygen production by pseudoplankton, that sort of thing." The drop of sweat rolled slowly down her forehead.

"What's going to happen with those, then?" I asked.

"I told you," she said. "We're still working on it."

"I heard you," I said. "But you must have some idea."

She swallowed. "So far, it doesn't look like there will be any serious disruption. After all, the atmosphere's *already* moving much faster than the surface."

The bead of sweat broke against an eyebrow, but another one had formed above it, back at the hairline. It's amazing how you notice things like that.

"But you're working on the basis of a sudden stop in rotation?" I asked. "Not a gradual one, or anything localized?"

"Yes," she said. She didn't nod.

I figured that she was giving me a pretty fair readout. "All right," I said. "I need to talk to whoever's in charge of the actual stop. Who is it?"

"That . . . that would be Doc Lee." She pointed vaguely to her left, moving her hand as little as possible.

I nodded. "Is this room private, or on open com?"

"I don't know," she said. It occurred to me that there was a hell of a lot she didn't know.

"Well, if it's on open com," I announced, "I want this Doc Lee to get down here and talk to me."

"I'm already here," a man's voice said, and a whole section of seascape vanished.

He was standing against the gray stone wall, tall and plump, with a scraggly black beard and, more importantly, with a gun in his hand. They *did* go armed in their own building, or at least they had weapons on hand. It wasn't an HG-2, just a little home security job, local manufacture; I knew the make, sold under three or four different names. It was not bright at all, even for a gun, and it usually carried tranks instead of anything fatal. I couldn't count on that, of course; it could use several kinds of ammunition. And it was a gun, pointed at me—other details weren't that important.

"You're Carlisle Hsing, aren't you?" he asked.

I was beginning to think that altogether too many people knew who I was. I decided not to answer.

"You must be," he said. "Paulie said you were poking around."

I still didn't answer, but I could see how he knew, anyway. There aren't that many people my size in the city.

Doc Lee, if that's who he was, shifted his grip on the gun and cleared his throat.

"Hsing," he said, "I think you'd better get out of here. You're trespassing, and I'm sure you're committing some sort of crime by pointing that thing of yours at this woman."

"I'm also getting some answers," I said.

"Not anymore. You fire that, and I'll drop you. You point it at me, and I'll drop you. I'll be acting in defense of myself and the Institute's property if I shoot you; if you fire, you're committing murder. Now, you get out of here peacefully and leave the Institute alone, and we'll forget all about this."

"I'm not forgetting about anything," I said. I put on my sincere approach. "Look, I need some answers from you people, and the gun's just the fastest way I could think of to pry them loose. Could we put away the hardware and just talk?"

"We've got nothing to talk about," he said, and he said it contemptuously. I didn't like that.

"I think we do," I said harshly. "Unless you want everything I know about the plans you and Nakada have for stopping the planet's rotation to be slapped onto every net in the city."

His gun wavered slightly, and I didn't think it was a software check.

"Want to put away the armament?" I asked again.

"No," he said, tightening up again. "If you put this on the nets, we'll ruin you."

"So what?" I said. "What the hell have I got to lose? If you know who I am, check out where and how I live, and how I got there, and what the hell, break into my financial records and take a look at those. You can't do anything to me that I can't do one hell of a lot worse to you. Now, are we going to talk?"

He hesitated, and the gun lowered slightly. "Not now. I need to think about this, talk it over with the others."

"All right," I said. "I can wait."

"I don't know how long it will take," he said.

"I'm in no hurry." I smiled at him.

"Listen," he said. "I can't leave you loose in the Institute, with that gun and your present attitude. Get out of here, go back to where you came from, and we'll call you, within . . . within twenty-four hours. If we don't, you go ahead and put whatever you want on the nets."

I considered that, and I didn't much like it. Anything could happen in twenty-four hours. They could fire off the big one and make all my questions moot. They could all be off-planet in an hour.

But it didn't look as if I was going to get him to tell me anything right there, and somebody might have called the cops already, or put something in the air that would take me right out, not to mention that he was quite right about what would happen if any triggers got pulled. I figured I could still dicker a little, but I couldn't fight.

"Two hours," I said. "And nobody leaves the city."

He glanced at the woman. "All right, two hours."

I nodded and backed out toward the street, with the HG-2 easy in my hand. "Nobody leaves the city," I repeated.

He nodded. "Nobody leaves."

I nodded back, and then I was out in the corridor; I turned and struggled not to run as I hurried to the door, feeling very, very exposed.

It wasn't a run, but it wasn't all that dignified, either. All the same, I got out before any cops or security machines got me, and that was the important part. I remembered to stop at the door and turn off the Sony-Remington and shove it back in its holster; then I stepped out of the shadows into the red glow of the night sky, and I called a cab.

Chapter Fourteen

BY THE TIME THE CAB LIFTED I WAS HAVING SECOND thoughts. I couldn't flag exactly where I'd screwed up, but I knew I had somewhere along the line. I didn't have enough control. I'd given Doc Lee and whoever else was involved two hours to come up with something, and that was at least an hour and fifty-five minutes too long.

But I didn't see what else I could have done. I hadn't had any time to waste, because the charges might already have been set, despite what Nakada said. I'd had to get into the Ipsy fast, and I hadn't seen any other way than with the gun. If I'd tried going in on wire I'd have hit high security—wouldn't I?

Maybe not, but I'd thought I would. I hadn't stopped to see if I was right, and maybe I should have.

Of course, maybe all the work was being done in human skulls and other closed systems, in which case I wouldn't have found anything even if I *had* gone in on wire.

Going in in person had seemed the only way. Using the

gun to get answers had seemed the best way. Nobody had ever called my bluff quite so completely before.

That made me wonder about this Doc Lee. I wasn't sure if I'd ever heard of him or not; he might have been on a couple of public affairs feeds, but I couldn't swear to it. Just who the hell was he? Was this idea of stopping the planet's rotation his? What was his position at the Ipsy?

I didn't know, and I knew that I should. I would have used the cab's terminal to see what I could get on him if I had had anything left on my card besides last-line bank credit.

Instead I forced myself to stop worrying about that particular detail for a moment while I looked around.

The Trap was big and bright and a million vivid colors out the cab's window on the right, the burbs mostly low and in dim shades of gray on the left. A line of advertisers squealed past overhead, but didn't target me; a spy-eye looked in, then turned away, obviously after someone else. The city was going about its business, just as it always had, and except for a handful, everybody in Nightside City was still expecting the city to die a slow, steady death with encroaching dawn.

I wasn't sure whether it was going to die slowly, or live, or die a fast and horrible death that would take me with it.

Worse, I wasn't sure whether I'd live to see whatever happened. If Lee was a hotshot at the Ipsy he might very well have some way of stopping my files from hitting the nets, even from the ITEOD banks. If he did, he'd have no reason to keep me alive, and although I'd never heard of Paulie Orchid doing anything as big-time as a permanent murder, I didn't think the little bastard would balk if Lee sent him to take me out. After all, Orchid was doing a lot of things now that I'd never have expected.

And even if Orchid did balk, there was the other muscle, the big guy—Rigmus, or whoever he was.

Suddenly I was scared as hell. I had screwed this one up *bad*, worse than when I let that welsher go.

Of course, it might all work out, I told myself. They might come through and tell me their whole plan, and it might be good and clean, and I might just settle down peacefully. Or it might be a disaster about to happen, and I might accept a little money to keep my mouth shut, enough to get off-planet, and then I might blow the horn on them anyway once I was clear—I didn't mind committing either blackmail or betrayal when the victims were planning mass murder.

But I was scared all the same that I had screwed up badly, and that I was going to pay for it.

I was right, too, but I didn't find that out right away.

The cab dropped me at my door, and I stepped out into the wind and looked around, just in case.

It looked clear. I didn't have anything with me that would scan much outside the visible, but it looked clear. The wind stung my eyes, and I blinked and opened the door.

Upstairs in my office I noticed that the window was still black, and I cleared it. If something came at me that way I wanted to see it—not that I expected any approach that obvious.

I also didn't mind looking out at the city again, seeing the flickering of the Trap and a swarm of meteors that drew golden clawmarks across the deep blue of the sky, hearing the hum of the traffic and the howl of the wind.

I got myself paté and crackers and a Coke III and I sat down at my desk and tried to think of what I could do with my two hours that could possibly be of use.

The obvious item was to run up a file on Doc Lee, so I touched keys.

His name was Mahendra Dhuc Lee, he was just over a hundred in Terran years, he'd been born on Prometheus, and he was assistant director of research in physical planetology, with a degree from Prometheus and a doctorate from Earth—I'd never heard of either university, so I won't name names. There was more, but it was dull as dirt; like most scientists, he'd never done anything but science and office politics, and either one is boring as hell to outsiders. He appeared to be good at both. Whether it was because he was good enough at both to offend people, or whether there was truth in it, I couldn't be sure, but there was a rumor that he'd been less than completely honest in some of his work—adjusting results to please backers, borrowing other people's work, the usual array of scientific misbehavior.

It looked to me as if he was someone who thought a lot of himself and always had, despite any evidence to the contrary. I figured that he'd gone into science not because he was good at it, or enjoyed it, but because he'd bought the line about science being the key to the future, the field for someone who wanted to really accomplish something.

Of course, he should have gone into polyspatial physics or something, then, instead of planetology; I'd bet that he picked planetology just because it had been his best subject.

I couldn't prove my guess, though, because his educational records weren't open.

I had another guess to make, which was that whatever he was working on for Nakada was intended to be his big score, his way of making his name and fortune, just the way it was for Nakada. Except he didn't have family and money supplying him with second chances; if he crashed on this one, that might be it for him.

I called for anything on his most recent work, but came

up blank. I had his basic biography, but details wouldn't come, just the outline.

That much, and a whole string of tedious interviews, were on the public records, available to anybody who asked. I wanted more than that, but I hesitated to go after it. I didn't know what security I might hit. I didn't know what might come after me. I didn't want to plug into the com when there might be somebody at my door any minute; it's hard to maneuver quickly with a wire fastened to the side of your head.

I put it aside and I finished my meal and I waited, and about fifteen minutes before the two hours would have been up I got a message beep.

I tapped keys, and Doc Lee's face came up on the screen.

"We've talked it over," he said, "and we've decided to trust you. We'll give you the full schematics for the whole project. In exchange, we want your word, with legal penalties attached, that you won't put any of this on the net until either full dawn or a halt in the city's sunward rotation, whichever comes first."

I stared at him. I couldn't believe it. Nothing had gone wrong after all. It seemed too good to be true.

"And no trespassing or assault charges?" I asked.

"No charges, either way," he said.

"All right," I said. "You've got a deal." I smiled at him to show that everything was running smooth and sweet. I felt good. I felt a rush of warmth, but I tried not to let it overwhelm me completely. I still thought there had to be a bug in the program somewhere.

"Here it comes, then," he said, and the screen filled with gobbledygook.

I tried to scan it, but it was moving too quickly, and I couldn't follow it.

"Wait a minute," I said. "Let me patch in some analysis. I can't read this that fast."

"If you'll jack on line," he told me, "we can feed everything right in with all the interpretation, and you can go through it and see if you have any questions."

I should have stopped to consider that, but I didn't. The cold little worm of disbelief was too deeply buried in all that warmth. I just nodded and jacked in and said, "Ready."

You've seen it coming, haven't you? Yeah, you're right. I got horsed. A classic Trojan horse.

I got the initial feed, good hard data on Epimetheus, Nightside City, all their various motions, the vectors needed to stop the city—and then I hit the neural breaker that cut my body out of the circuit and left me hooked into the system with no way to move my hand and unplug.

They left the sensory input alone; nothing went but motor control. The bastards knew just what they were doing.

I'd always known that running on wire was dangerous. That was what I was telling myself, over and over, but it didn't do any good. They had me locked on data reception, on an indefinite hold awaiting transmission, and of course they weren't sending any transmission.

That sudden cooperation had been too good to be true, all right. Something that seems too good to be true is a pretty sure sign of a con, and I've always known that. I'd fallen right into it, all the same, because I had *wanted* it to be true.

I sat there like that, staring at the gigo on the screen, for maybe ten minutes; then the door buzzed as somebody ran an override on it. It opened, and the muscle came in.

Big and little, just the way the squatters had described them, and yes, the little one was Paulie Orchid. He was smiling and rubbing his palms together.

The big one was some guy I had never seen before, huge and middling ugly, with a face like a potato that had flunked the port health check, and dirty blond hair that had been hacked off short and left for dead. He looked worried, and when he stepped closer I heard his stomach growl. He had a coil of cable in one hand.

Orchid took the cable, then bent down and kissed my cheek. I'd have spat at him if I'd been able to move.

"Hello, Carlie," he said. "Didn't I tell you to mind your own business?" He smiled. "No answer? Feeling shy? Here, give me your hand."

He reached down and picked my right hand off the keyboard, and I felt my stomach heave. On top of the emotional sine curve I'd been riding, from terror to the relief of Lee's lies and then back into terror when I got horsed, just seeing these two in my office was enough to make me sick. Having that piece of grit touch me and move me around like a toy was too much. Antiperistalsis is not under the control of the voluntary nervous system; I threw my lunch up on his arm.

He jumped back, and I saw the big one smother a smile.

Orchid must have known the smile was there, though, because without looking he said, "Shut up, Bobo." He snarled it, more than said it; it sounded like bad brakes on a matatu. "Damn, now we have to clean this up." He slapped me across the face but pulled it at the last instant—I guess he didn't want to leave a permanent mark, though I don't know why he'd worry about that. It still hurt like hell.

"I'd been thinking of having a bit of fun with you, while you're out of service," he said. "Something to make this more enjoyable for both of us. But you—you've spoiled my appetite for that." He grimaced. "I didn't think anything could do that."

"Besides, Paulie," the other one, Bobo, said, "if she

could still puke while she's under, think what her cunt might do. I've heard about stuff like that, involuntary stuff."

Orchid glanced at him. He didn't answer, but he'd obviously heard about stuff like that, too.

Knowing I wasn't about to be raped did damn little for my peace of mind, though.

They ignored me for a few minutes while they found the necessaries and got the mess tidied away. When that was done they didn't waste any more time on talk; Orchid yanked me out of my chair by my hands, dumped me on the floor, then pulled my hands behind me and tied them together. He tied my legs, stuffed a gag in my mouth, then reached inside my jacket and got my gun out. He dropped it on the desk. That left me pretty helpless even if I could move; he reached down, pulled the plug out of my socket, and stood back.

I flexed, glad to be back in control of myself, but Orchid had known what he was doing when he tied me up; I couldn't feel any slack anywhere.

Bobo picked me up and slung me over his shoulder.

I was wondering, the whole time, just what they had in mind. They obviously weren't just going to shoot me, or they'd have done it already instead of tying me up.

I also wondered how thorough they'd been in taking out my security systems. Not that I had anything high-powered, you understand, but I wondered what was going to happen to my files, both on site and in the ITEOD banks. I wondered whether the overridden door had recorded their entry.

I wondered if I'd be around to find out.

Bobo hefted me. "She don't weigh much of anything." His stomach growled again, and I thought he winced a bit—I wondered if he had some sort of digestive problem, something his symbiote couldn't deal with.

Not that I really cared if he fell dead from internal bleeding, you understand, but I'm just that sort of person, curious by nature.

They took me down to the street and dumped me into a cab they had waiting there. It didn't say a word, and the upholstery felt dead. I twisted around for a look at it.

The cab was an old one, not very well kept up, and they clearly hadn't just picked it at random on their way in. The core access panel was open, and I could see that the motherboard had been cracked across, right through the crystal at the center; they'd killed the cab's brain. I hoped that it hadn't been one of the more self-aware ones; bad enough that my mistakes were getting *me* shut down, without taking innocents with me.

Poor maintenance, though, usually meant an independent, and a cab can't buy itself free unless it's sentient. I decided not to think about that any further, not just then. I had enough to worry about on my own account.

Bobo held me down on the seat with one hand while Orchid leaned over and poked at the exposed circuitry. He made a connection, then pulled back. "Okay, that's got it."

Nodding, Bobo pulled a needle from his pocket and jabbed under my jaw with it.

I felt it go in, and then I felt a spreading numbness. I didn't know if it was a bug or a drug or what, but it was obviously something designed to put me out for a while.

I wondered why they hadn't dosed me back in my office, and decided that it was pure sadism on Orchid's part. He wanted me awake and aware of my helplessness for as long as possible. Maybe he even wanted me to see what they'd done to the poor cab.

I was starting to get fuzzy, but I felt Bobo cut the cables

from my ankles and wrists, and I thought I saw him throw them out on the street. I started to turn, but I was fading fast, and before I could get myself running clean the door had closed, with me still inside. I tried to fall against the door, and maybe I did, but it didn't open.

Then I lost it completely, and I don't remember a damn thing of what happened for a long time after that.

Chapter Fifteen

I WOKE UP WITH A HORRIBLE YELLOW GLARE IN MY face; the instant my eyes opened I reconsidered and closed them again. Even then, the darkness was blood red instead of cool black, and I realized I was looking at the insides of my eyelids.

My skin felt dry and crawling, and the wind was screaming much more audibly than usual, and at a higher pitch. I'd never heard anything like it. It was the only sound; there was no music, no background hum at all. I had a gnawing suspicion that I wasn't in the city anymore.

I didn't want to think about where I was instead. That blast of light was a pretty clear indication, but I didn't want to think about that.

With my eyes still shut I felt around and discovered inert upholstery on all sides. I stretched and found that I could move freely; I wasn't tied, wasn't confined in anything very small. Something was in my mouth, though— the gag Orchid had stuffed in. I reached up, pulled it out, and tossed it aside.

152

I flexed my right arm; it was still slightly sore from the recoil when I had taken out the spy-eye. My wrists and ankles were a bit chafed, and my mouth was dry. I thought I might still be feeling a trace of whatever had put me under, as well. Other than that, I seemed to be all there and reasonably sound.

That seemed to be about all I could do with my eyes closed. I put my hands over them and opened them a slit.

That wasn't too bad. If I squinted and blinked a lot, I thought I could manage. I moved my hands a little, so I could peek through my fingers.

I was still in the cab. It wasn't moving. It was lying on the ground, cocked at an odd angle. One door was slightly sprung, which I figured would account for the wind noise. Other than that it looked pretty much as I remembered it; the access panel was still open, bare circuitry showing. The seats were inert, the screens all dark, the readouts all blank, and not even the system-failure lights were still glowing—at least, not that I could see in the glare.

All the colors seemed wrong because of the light, but I didn't doubt for a minute that I was still in the same cab I'd passed out in.

The entire upper bubble was transparent, though, and the scenery outside wasn't anywhere in Nightside City. It wasn't on the nightside at all. The entire sky was a blindingly bright pale blue that was almost white; I knew it wasn't really white only because it was streaked with thin, high, fast-moving clouds that *were* really white. That sky was terrifyingly alien, awash in more light than I had thought the universe could hold.

The only other thing I could see, in any direction, was bare ground, and that ground was sand and rock—gray sand, black rock, mostly, with streaks of brown here and there. It stretched off to an impossibly distant horizon. I'd lived my whole life at the bottom of a crater; I'd never seen a real horizon before, except in vids, and all that openness was absolutely terrifying. Nothing stood between me and the rest of the universe but open plain.

And light blazed off everything, intense white light, blinding light, brilliant light. It sparkled off the sands, off the rocks; it prismed rainbows off the cab's bubble.

It was beautiful, in a painful sort of way. I'd seen light that bright, in a small area, for a moment or two, but to see an entire vast landscape, from one horizon to the other, ablaze in that glare—it was a new experience for me, and one that I couldn't help but appreciate, despite my sorry situation.

I knew, though, that my situation was bad. The bubble might provide a little protection—though probably not, since there was no need for any such protection on the nightside—but I knew the sun's ultraviolet had probably already done a good bit of skin damage, and maybe eye damage as well. I might be dying; I might already be in desperate need of medical treatment.

And of course, I wasn't about to get that treatment. I had no idea where the hell I was, except that it was on the dayside—since I was in the same cab, I had to assume I was still on Epimetheus. I knew I couldn't count on planetary rotation bringing me the safety of night any time soon.

If I wanted the night, I'd have to go to it; it wouldn't come to me.

It was pretty clear that nobody was going to come and get me, either; I'd have to get back to the nightside on my own. Nobody kept track of me. Nobody would notice I was missing until it was too late. My only family on the planet was my brother 'Chan—he called maybe once every four or five weeks, and his last call had been a week ago. I still had a few friends, but if they noticed at all, they wouldn't worry if I didn't answer calls or show up at Lui's for a few days; I'd done that before, when I was working or busy or just depressed.

I wondered whether anybody might miss the cab and come looking for it, but then I dismissed the idea. I'd already noticed, before I passed out, that it looked like an independent, and a glance at the hardcopy license and ownership statement next to the passenger readout screen confirmed that. This cab had been as much a loner as I was, bought free from Q.Q.T. over a year ago.

I looked up from the statement to that open access panel and all the obviously dead inboard systems, and I shuddered at the thought that I might have to get out and *walk* in the sunlight.

That wasn't certain yet, though. I leaned forward and poked around a little.

The motherboard was snapped in two, and the central processor, the brain, was crushed; the cab itself was dead, beyond any possible doubt. I prodded a few other systems. None of them were working, but most of them looked intact, and after all, the poor lobotomized thing had probably flown here under its own power. If Orchid and Rigmus—I figured Bobo had to be Bobo Rigmus, of course—had been able to make the corpse fly, I thought maybe I could, too. There had to be a patched-in slave program somewhere that had worked the drives.

I couldn't get any current anywhere, though. Something had cut the power feed. At first I didn't think that was necessarily irreparable.

Then I got past the firewall and got a look at the main power plant.

They'd put some sort of timed charge on it, I guess. However they'd arranged it, one whole side was blown out.

Fortunately for me, it was a side that faced away from the passenger compartment; otherwise I'd have been dead, which was probably what they had intended. They probably expected the whole thing to blow, which would leave me as just a little more radioactive debris. Instead, I was alive, but I'd probably caught a good dose of radiation all the same, and that side of the cab had probably left a streak of hot dust for a dozen kilometers before the poor thing hit ground.

The power plant was just scrap now, which meant that the cab obviously wasn't going anywhere, but I'd survived. I'd bought myself a slow death instead of a quick one.

Or had I?

I was having trouble taking it all in—everything was so alien that I couldn't just accept it as it appeared and go on from there. I had to think it through.

Just what had happened?

Obviously, Paulie Orchid and Bobo Rigmus had taken me and stuck me in a sabotaged cab and sent me out onto the dayside to die. But why?

I could make a pretty good guess. If I had turned up dead in the city, inquiries would have been made. My ITEOD records would have been pulled, and although they weren't as complete and up-to-date as I might have liked, they'd show that Sayuri Nakada and the Ipsy were up to something, and that I had been investigating that.

Somebody would be able to put the clues together, and the whole scheme would have been crashed.

But if I just *disappeared*, none of that would happen. At least, not for some time, not until somebody realized how long I had been gone. It could take weeks, maybe longer. And when it did show up, nobody would be sure I was dead; my ITEOD records would remain sealed until somebody got a court order. And nobody was likely to bother with that.

Nobody was going to find me there on the dayside. My body would just dry up and weather away.

And if they *did* find me, me and the cab, there would be no hard evidence that it was murder, that it hadn't been a bizarre and inexplicable accident or a particularly weird suicide.

It was a pretty damn good way of disposing of me, really. It got around the ITEOD files nicely. I had to admit that. I wondered who had thought of it. I'd have picked Doc Lee if I had to guess.

But *why*? Clever or not, why did they bother? Why was I so great a threat that they were ready to go to all this trouble to kill me secretly, rather that just telling me what was going on?

I didn't know, and there in the cab I didn't see any way of finding out. All I knew was that they had sent me out here to die.

But I had no intention of dying. Aside from all the usual reasons—and I'd say my survival instinct is as strong as anybody's—I didn't want to give them the satisfaction. I sure as hell wasn't going to give up without a fight. I tapped my wrist and said, "I need a cab, or an ambulance or patrol car; this is an emergency."

My voice was a croak. The gag had soaked up all the moisture in my mouth, and the dry air in the cab was making it hard to recover.

My transceiver did nothing. No beep. If it had heard my command and tried to obey, it hadn't been able to get an acknowledgment from anyone.

I swallowed, got my mouth working a little better, and tried again.

"I said, cab, please!" This time it came out clear and angry.

The transceiver buzzed, an ugly, negative sound. It had tried. It hadn't gotten through. Nobody was in range.

I was hot, I realized, hot and tired—my little doze on the way east hadn't really left me well rested. I was scared bad, too. My wrist was shaking as I looked at the skin covering the transceiver, and sweat shone in a thin film.

And I hadn't done anything yet, hadn't gone anywhere. I'd only been awake for a few minutes.

I looked up, then wished I hadn't; that blue-white sky was one huge glare.

I looked down again and around at what I could see.

There was nothing else in the cab I could use. The transmitters might not be smashed like the motherboard and the power plant, but I had no juice for them; I didn't have any way to rig an adapter for my body current, and that probably wouldn't have been enough anyway. It apparently wasn't enough for my wrist transceiver.

Hell, I was probably below the broadcast horizon for the city anyway. I'd have a better chance of contacting ships in space. Except that most ships don't come over the dayside anywhere below high orbit, and they wouldn't be listening on ground-use frequencies.

I was stranded. Barring miracles, my only way out was to walk back to the nightside.

I wasn't too picky about just *where* on the nightside. Anywhere would do; most of the nightside is at least borderline habitable, and the bad spots are mostly pretty far back from the terminator. I didn't think I'd be lucky enough to hit Nightside City right off, but if I reached the twilight zone and then turned and kept walking along the terminator, I thought I ought to hit either the city or a working mine camp, and miners could get me to the city.

First, though, I had to get to the terminator, and I had no idea how far that might be. The sun didn't seem very high in the sky, and the shadows were long—but Epimetheus is a good-sized planet, as I've said before. Great-circle circumference is 28,500 kilometers, more or less.

With Nightside City on the terminator, that put it roughly seven thousand kilometers from the noon pole. I wasn't *that* far, obviously, but looking in the general direction of the sun—I couldn't look right *at* it, of course—I could easily have been one or two thousand kilometers east of the terminator.

That's one hell of a long walk.

But what choice did I have?

Waiting wasn't going to do me any good, either. A journey of a thousand kilometers begins with a single step, right? It was time to stop dawdling and take that first step.

With no power available I had to kick open the sprung door to get out, and the instant my foot knocked it loose the wind, which I had already thought was screaming, became an ear-wracking shriek. It filled the little cab with a whirlwind, whipping dust into rising coils; the core access panel flapped clumsily, in a broken rhythm like an old blues riff.

I'd forgotten about that. I'd forgotten the wind.

In Nightside City, the wind isn't that bad. It's always there, and it can eat at your nerves and snatch at your clothes and carry things away if you don't hold them down, but it's not that bad. Generally speaking, top speed is maybe sixty, seventy kilometers an hour.

But that's because the city's in a crater, and the crater walls block the *real* winds. The *lowest* wind speed ever recorded on the surface of Epimetheus, excluding craters and the four poles, is a hundred kilometers per hour. It peaks at a hundred and fifty.

And it never stops. Never. Never lets up at all.

It's because of the slow rotation and the generally smooth surface. With the mantle still semiliquid, or at least pretty soft, and the continental plates as small as they are, Epimetheus doesn't have a lot of big mountains; they sink back in or get eroded away almost as fast as they form. The only reason the city's crater is stable is that it's smack in the middle for a plate, where it's balanced and doesn't tip. Whatever made the crater wasn't going fast enough to punch right through the crust. It's a fluke. It's a temporary fluke, too, because the wall is wearing away—but that takes time. It'll happen, though. All the active wind and water and even the steady spray of celestial debris help keep the surface level, wearing away any mountains or craters that do form.

Anyway, ignoring the flukes, most of the planet's smooth and flat, with nothing to stop the wind.

As for how the winds got started, that's where the slow rotation comes in. At the noon pole, which is over an ocean and has been for as long as humans have been on the planet, the sun heats the air, and it rises, carrying water vapor, and it blows away nightward at high altitude. The air cools along the way and drops the water as rain in the rainbelt, starting about two hundred kilometers past the terminator onto the nightside. At the midnight pole all that cool air drops down to the slushcap and blows back dayward along the ground, back toward the noon pole.

It's one huge convection current, that's all. One great big convection current that covers the entire planet. And in the millions of years since the planet's rotation slowed enough for there to *be* a noon pole and a midnight pole, it's worked up to be a pretty good speed.

What this really means is that the entire atmosphere of Epimetheus is one big windstorm, one that's been going on for millions of years and will go on for millions more.

That added a nice little final touch to my position; I had to walk a thousand kilometers or more head-on into that wind, that hundred-kilometer-an-hour wind.

But I didn't have any choice, so I took a look around the cab, picked up the discarded gag, decided there wasn't anything else of any possible use, and then I slid out the door onto the hard gray sand and I started walking into that wind, head down, jacket pulled up around my neck, with the sun hot on my back and the skin on my hands already red with sunburn, almost starting to blister. I wrapped the gag, which was a strip of porous fabric I couldn't identify, across my mouth to make breathing easier.

The wind almost lifted me from the ground with every step; it was a constant pressure fighting me. I turned first one shoulder forward, then the other, to cut into the wind, and that helped a little. If I stopped moving and stayed upright, I knew it would blow me back east like an empty wrapper down an alley, probably at twice the speed I made by walking.

I wished I was heavier, but I wasn't, and I wasn't going to get any heavier.

About a kilometer from the cab my grip on the gag slipped, and the wind snatched the cloth away and sent it sailing eastward. I turned for a second to watch it go, but I never considered trying to retrieve it; it was moving faster than I ever could, and in the wrong direction.

I turned westward again and marched on, making do without it.

At least I always knew which way to go; face to the wind, walking up my own shadow, away from the sun.

That shadow—that was something of a new experience, too, having a shadow stretched out before me, that moved when I moved, but that always kept the same shape. I'd seen plenty of shadows and cast my share, but when I walked in front of a light in the city my shadow would shorten, then lengthen, as I walked past. Eta Cass B cast shadows, of course, but they were faint things, just darker patches in the red darkness of the city streets. Eta Cass A wasn't so gentle; that shadow before me was hard-edged and sharp, black against the glowing sands.

The shadow was my own little piece of the night, and I

admired it as I walked—when I could bear to open my eyes and look at it.

I had hoped, when I left the cab, that the wind would be cool, but it was too hard to feel cool; it didn't soothe, it ripped and tore, and I felt my skin tightening against it. I squinted against the wind and the glare, sometimes closing my eyes entirely. I didn't need to see to keep the right direction, only to keep from stumbling over the rocks that dotted the plain.

I hoped that my symbiote was handling the ultraviolet and the windburn, but I knew that it probably couldn't. It was meant for cuts and scrapes, the odd infection, general tissue maintenance—not for fending off the constant assault of a hurricane or hard radiation.

The wind stole my sweat away as fast as it emerged, and I was dry and thirsty within twenty paces, and although I still didn't feel cool, I was shivering with an uncontrollable chill before I'd walked the cab under the horizon.

But I walked on. What else could I do?

The thought that I might be on the wrong side of a sea occurred to me pretty much right at the start, too, but there wasn't anything I could do about that, either. I just walked.

I had no choice unless I wanted to just lie down and die. I didn't. I walked.

It was a waking nightmare. At times I felt as dead as Orchid and Rigmus surely thought I already was, but I never stopped. I'm not someone who could ever just lie down and die, not while I could still move. I had no food, no water, but with my symbiote to help, I thought I could last as much as a week—I had paid extra, back when I could afford it, to get a symbiote with a transferable energy reserve, and with the capability to digest excess tissue in a really bad emergency. Like this one. I figured that I had a week, but that at the end of that time I'd have no fat, no appendix, and maybe less tissue on several organs.

To walk a thousand kilometers in a week I needed to cover a hundred and forty-three a day, about six every hour—no sleep at all, of course. I couldn't afford to sleep. Six kilometers an hour didn't seem that much, just a fast walk.

A fast walk in blazing sun into a hundred-kilometer-an-hour headwind, nonstop for seven days.

I think I knew it was hopeless right from the first.

But I had no choice.

I don't know how long I walked, or how far. My landmarks weren't by distance or time, since I had no way of measuring either one. My landmarks were signs of progress or impending doom.

The signs of progress were few and feeble: losing sight of the cab, or imagining that my shadow had lengthened a bit. The signs of impending doom were another matter.

There were the blisters that formed on the backs of my hands, and then the blisters on the back of my neck, and in time the blisters on my feet that probably weren't from the sun at all, but from walking too much.

There was the first time I stumbled over a rock, and the first time I stumbled and fell, and the first time I fell and couldn't get up right away.

There was the time when the grit in the wind finally ruined the seal on my jacket, so it wouldn't hold any longer.

There was the time I threw away my empty holster, to save weight, and the time not long after that when I wondered if chewing on it might have yielded a trace of moisture.

There was the time when I realized that my eyes were *not* just adjusting to the glare, but that my vision was fading—the ultraviolet had burned my retinas. I saw the sand as just an expanse of gray, rather than individual grains.

In time, I no longer saw the smaller rocks, and the fine details of the sky—the high, lacy clouds blowing fiercely westward, outracing me on their way to the rainbelt—vanished into a white blur.

My mind wandered, of course. Walking across that wasteland, all of it the same, the details fading as my eyesight faded, how could I possibly keep all my attention on what I was doing?

I tried to imagine what a sea would look like if I hit one—assuming I could still see and didn't walk right into it. I'd seen holos, of course, and even direct visual feeds off wire of nightside seas, but I didn't remember a wire feed of a daytime sea, and holos don't always capture everything. That bright daylight would sparkle from the water, I knew, but I couldn't remember just what the holos had looked like, whether they had shown daylight lancing painfully, the way it glinted from some of the rocks, or whether the water muted it somehow. I thought the pseudoplankton might absorb some of the light.

I wondered if Epimethean seawater would kill me quickly, or only slowly, if I drank it. I knew that it was toxic. The seas were radioactive and rich in metal salts.

I knew that if I reached a sea, I would try to drink the water. My thirst was completely beyond rational control. The thought of drinking my own blood occurred to me, and if I'd had a good sharp blade I might have tried it, but with nothing sharp except my teeth I was able to resist.

I wondered whether my little stroll would have been better or worse if Epimetheus had native life on land, and decided that it would depend on just what kind of life, but that it would probably be worse. After all, the pseudoplankton were toxic—as toxic as the seas they lived in, maybe more so; laced with heavy metals, their whole biochemistry based on heavy metals—and any land life would have to be equally poisonous, wouldn't it?

But then, if Epimetheus had had trees, they might have cut the wind a little. I felt as if microscopic grit was being rammed into my skin with every step I took into the perpetual gale, and the idea of a drop in wind speed came pretty close to paradise just then. So maybe trees, even poisonous trees with tempting, lethal fruit, would have been an improvement.

Animals, though—animals were something I didn't want. Not that I had to worry about those, since the planet had never evolved any, even in the seas. The idea of alien, untailored organisms scampering about was unpleasant. I didn't like things that much out of control. I didn't like the idea of things that could sneak up on me, things I knew nothing about.

I knew that there were no native animals on Epimetheus, but I thought about them anyway. I thought about things prowling behind me, just out of sight, the sound of their movements lost in the wind. I began to imagine that they were really there.

The fact that I was losing my sight made those imaginings worse. I never liked things I couldn't see, and as I struggled on I could see less and less, as if that whole blazing bright world were vanishing into a hot mist.

I hated that.

When I was a girl, a very young girl, it still rained in Nightside City sometimes. The crater was already east of the rainbelt when I was born, but there were flukes, bits and pieces of clouds that dropped down out of the upper flow and were sent eastward again without ever reaching the main body of the rainbelt. Some of those happened to hit the city's crater, and if they were still high enough to clear the western wall, we got rain. I remember that rain. Fat raindrops would come splashing down from the sky, sending ripples of distortion through the advertising displays, drawing streaks on the black glass walls, forming puddles on the street that would turn slick and green with pseudoplankton in minutes. Most of my friends didn't like it and stayed inside, but I loved it. I would go out barefoot in the streets, running through the puddles, trying to splash them dry before they could turn green, feeling the rain in my hair and on my back and rolling down inside the collar of my coverall. I would stop and stand and look up at the sky, mouth open, feeling the rain on my face and staring in wonder at a sky without stars, without the red glow of Eta Cass B, but with a gray cap on it that reflected back the city's lights as a warm, even shimmer.

When I got home after the rain had stopped my father always shouted at me that I was a fool to behave like that; that if I kept my mouth open long enough in the rain, the pseudoplankton might just start growing in *me*. I laughed at him. I thought that was just silly. I knew the rain wouldn't hurt me. It was clean and cool and wonderful; it couldn't hurt me.

I think I was maybe six years old, Terran years, when it really rained for the last time. Once or twice after that a wisp of cloud drifted in from somewhere, but it brought mist, not rain. The cloud wouldn't be thick enough to break into rain; instead it would settle down into the city streets as mist, as fog, wrapping haloes around every light and hiding the edges and angles on everything.

The soft blurring frightened me, where my father's threats about pseudoplankton only amused me, and I didn't go out in the fog. If you walked in the mist, you could feel the droplets on your skin, wet and cool, but they weren't distinct impacts, each drop a unit, the way the rain had been. Instead the mist was like a soft sheet, brushing over you but never coming to rest, never staying where you could get hold of it.

I didn't like that. I liked my reality hard-edged. I didn't

mind if it was messy, like the dead green scabs left by dried puddles, like the tangle of advertising and counter-advertising in Trap Over, like some of the work I had done for the casinos before they threw me out, or had done for myself since. I didn't mind if it was messy, but I wanted to see it all clearly. I wanted to know what I was feeling.

The mist terrified me. I didn't mind the rain. I never minded the rain.

I wished I could see rain again right then, as I was staggering across the dry, barren sands where rain hadn't fallen in millennia, with my vision fading into blackness while the sun still beat down on my back. I wanted to stand there with my mouth open to the sky, laughing at the idea that anything harmful could get at me.

I wasn't laughing. It wasn't raining. There wasn't even a cool mist, but a hot one, a mist of dust and wind and blinding sunlight—literally blinding, bright with that ghastly unseen ultraviolet that was stealing my vision. I couldn't see anything but a hot blur anymore, couldn't feel anything but the wind ripping at my raw sunburnt skin. Someone had gotten at me. Someone had gotten at me and sent me out into the daylight to shrivel and die, lost and blind.

And I didn't really even know why. I didn't know why I had to die rather than be allowed to find out what was happening.

It didn't make any sense.

I staggered on, and on, and on, always into the wind.

Chapter Sixteen

I DON'T REMEMBER WHEN I FINALLY FELL AND COULDN'T get up. I don't know when it happened, or how far I'd gone. I know I was blind by then, and that my skin had peeled off in layers leaving me raw and red on every exposed surface, and that my feet were numb and the slippers of my worksuit were full of blood. I assumed that my symbiote had suppressed most of the pain for as long as it could, but I was in agony all the same—but numb at the same time. After a certain point, physical pain doesn't have any real effect anymore; the emotions overload and just tune it out.

I don't remember the fall, but I was face down in that hard gray sand, and I knew that this time I wouldn't get up again. I was beyond trying. I couldn't face the wind again.

But I still couldn't let go and die.

I tapped my wrist, wincing at the pain of my own touch on the raw flesh, and tried to call for a cab; I don't know if I really thought I might be back in range, or whether I just didn't know what else to do.

It doesn't matter; I couldn't get the words out. My throat felt choked with sand.

And after that I don't remember anything at all from my stay on the dayside. My next memory is of lying on my back on something cool and slick that shaped itself to my body. I couldn't see anything, but my skin felt cool and moist and nothing hurt. I heard music instead of wind. I remember lying like that for a long moment and then falling asleep.

When I woke up—and I don't know if it was the next time, or if there had been other wakeful periods that never made it into long-term memory—my eyes stung and felt curiously clean and spare, as if all the accumulated gunk had been blasted away, leaving only the live tissue. I opened them and discovered that I could see as well as ever.

I was looking up at a beige ceiling. Soft music was playing, almost subliminal.

"Whoo," I said, not a word, just a noise. My voice worked, though it was dry and thin.

I heard someone move, and I tried to turn my head, and that made me woozy for a moment. When I could focus again I saw my brother's face.

Sebastian Hsing was looking down at me with that same irritating perpetual calm he'd always had.

"Hello, Carlie," he said. "What the hell did you get yourself into this time?"

He was the one person on Epimetheus who could still call me Carlie if he wanted, and I wouldn't mind a bit. I think I smiled at him—or tried to.

I swallowed some of that dryness in my throat and raised a hand to gesture. "Nothing serious," I said. I swallowed again and then added, "It's good to see you, 'Chan."

He made a bark of amused annoyance. "I can think of better places to see you," he said.

"I suppose so," I said. "Where am I, anyway?"

"You're in the hospital, stupid," he retorted. "Where'd you think?"

I tried to shrug, but it didn't work very well.

"I don't know," I said. I tried to change the subject. "Heard anything from Ali lately?"

He shook his head. "Not much. She made it to Earth, I guess; at least, I got a datatab from her postmarked on Earth, but it was blank. Don't know what happened to it; maybe it got wiped, maybe she forgot to record anything in the first place, maybe she mailed the wrong tab."

I didn't know what had happened either, but whatever it was didn't surprise me. Our kid sister Alison was never very good at staying in touch—but then, none of us were. At least Ali had gotten off Epimetheus.

I hadn't managed that, but I'd gotten off the nightside.

"How'd you find me?" I asked.

"I didn't," he said. "They called me because I'm your next of kin, but it wasn't me who found you."

I waited for him to go on, but he didn't. I pushed myself up on my elbows and demanded, "Well, then who the hell *did* find me?"

'Chan smiled and pointed. "Him," he said.

I turned, and there in a doorway opposite the foot of the bed was a huge, ugly man. For a moment I thought it was Bobo Rigmus, that he'd had an attack of contrition or something, but then I saw the black hair and smooth face and the three silver antennae trailing back from his left ear.

"Who—" I began, and then something about that face registered. "Mishima?"

He nodded. It was Big Jim Mishima, all right. I'd seen him on the com half a dozen times during the years we'd both worked the detective racket in the city. We hadn't met in person, not even over the Starshine Palace case, but here he was.

"Hello, Hsing," he said. "You owe me a lot of money. A *lot* of money. You shot my eye, and even after you did that, out of the kindness of my heart, I brought you back to the city. And I paid your bills here at the hospital, too."

"What the hell did you do that for?" I demanded.

"Because if you died, you wouldn't pay me back for the eye," he said, with a big fat smile on his big fat face.

I started to say something else, but one of my elbows slipped, and I fell back on the bed and decided against continuing the conversation.

Nobody argued with that decision, or if they did, I was too out of things to notice.

I woke up again feeling almost intact, but this time nobody human was in the room.

I wondered if I'd dreamed my chat with 'Chan and Mishima. I pushed myself up into a sitting position; the bed came up after me, so I figured I wasn't disobeying hospital orders.

The room was standard issue—four walls, a door, a nice relaxing holo of a park somewhere covering one wall, soothing music, and an assortment of display screens and gadgetry covering the wall at the head of the bed, all done in restful beige and cream.

I was about to call for word on my status when the door opened and Mishima came in.

"Hello, Hsing," he said again.

"Hello, Mishima," I answered.

"Before you ask," he said, "they tell me that you're fit to be released, but that you should take it easy for a while. And there's something important you should know, before you go anywhere." He paused, uneasily, I thought, and then finished. "Your symbiote's dead."

"It is?" I asked, startled. I hadn't expected that. Symbiotes are hard to kill, after all; they thrive on toxins of every sort. That's one reason people have them.

"So they tell me," Mishima said. "I guess the radiation got it."

I put a hand up, planning to run my fingers through my hair, but there wasn't any hair there.

Mishima noticed the gesture. "You took a *lot* of radiation, Hsing," he told me. "Not just the ultraviolet or the rest of the solar spectrum, either. You walked across some very hot ground, including the debris from your cab's power plant. They've flushed and rebuilt everything, so you're clean now; they regrew your skin, your bone marrow, just about everything that was damaged. Your hair and nails will grow back, and everything else already has, but it wasn't cheap, and I wasn't going to spring for a new symbiote on top of everything else. That's *your* problem."

I nodded. I could accept it. He didn't have to apologize for anything. Hell, the important thing was that *I* was alive; I'd never exactly been buddies with my symbiote. I'd been glad to have it, certainly; it had been comforting knowing it was there, but it wasn't sentient—some are, but mine wasn't—and I could get another. "Fair enough," I said. "Now would you mind explaining just how I got here, and why you're here talking to me?"

He pulled a chair from the wall; it shaped itself up and he settled onto it. "I'll tell you the whole thing," he said, "but I'll want some answers in exchange."

"What sort of answers?" I asked.

"Everything," he said. "Everything you were doing, how you got out on the dayside, all of it."

I guess I should have expected that, but I hadn't. I had to think it over for a moment.

It didn't take long. Whatever his reasons or methods, Mishima had saved my life. We were stuck with each other until that got balanced out somehow. "All right," I said, "You first."

So he told me.

He'd originally had the spy-eye cruising the Trap just in hopes of picking up something interesting. It had me on file, just in case I showed up, as something interesting. Mishima had put me in there long ago, right after the Starshine Palace case, and then forgotten about it. The file told the eye to see what I was up to, if I came by, and to let me know that Mishima didn't want me in the Trap. That was just as I'd figured it.

But when I actually *did* turn up in the Trap after so long and then gave the eye the dodge at the Manhattan, when he hadn't heard of anyone hiring me for anything, Mishima got curious about just what I was up to. He didn't have anything big on, and he thought I just might, so he told the eye to stick with me and find out what I was doing, and it tried.

He got some vague idea of what I was up to when I went out to the West End, but it wasn't clear. He didn't see what sort of a case I could have that involved tracking down rent collectors.

And then I crashed the eye, shooting it for no apparent reason except that it might find out where I was going, and he decided that whatever I was doing had to be a hell of a lot more interesting and important than strong-arming welshers for the Ginza, which was his main source of income at that point.

He was out an eye, but he wasn't about to let that slow him down. He bought himself some tracerized microintelligences and had a messenger dump them all over the street in front of my office. He put another eye on me, a top-of-the-line camouflaged high-altitude job that he had to put on credit because he'd already blown his budget.

He didn't see where I went after I shot the first eye; he picked me up again when I was back at my office, giving Doc Lee his two hours—not that Mishima knew that that was what it was. He saw two guys go into my place, then bring me out trussed up like a defective genen. He saw the butchered cab take off and head due east, barely clearing the crater wall.

But he lost me somewhere over the dayside. His eye couldn't take the UV and the wind and the heat.

The tracers should have been all over me, though, so he hired himself a ship and went looking. He found the cab, which still had some tracers in it, and they'd managed to assemble into a strong enough group for his equipment to pick up the signal, but I wasn't there. The wind had blown my tracks away, so he couldn't follow visually, either.

He was too damn stubborn to quit, though. He knew I'd gotten out of the cab alive, and he figured I'd head west, since anything else would have been completely idiotic, and he started running search patterns.

And obviously, since I'm here telling you this, he found me.

But do you want to know what led him to me? It wasn't the tracers; my symbiote had decided they were benign, but it had eaten them anyway because it needed the fuel, so they never got a transmitter built. He didn't find me visually, with all that dayside glare in equipment that had been designed for the nightside, and my heat signature got lost in the sunlight, indistinguishable from a stray rock.

It was when I tried to call for a cab right before I passed out. The transceiver had a safety feature I didn't even know about, and when I tapped and neither called nor cancelled, it checked my pulse, and when that came up weak it called for medical help. The only receiver in range was aboard Mishima's ship, and it picked up the call and told Big Jim.

He figured it had to be me. I had to be the only person on the dayside who could be calling for help. And besides, even if it wasn't me, refusing to answer a medical emergency call can get a ship's operating license pulled.

So he found me there, unconscious, half-buried in drifting sand, my skin in sunburnt shreds, blind, with a bad case of radiation poisoning—besides the stuff from the cab I'd walked right across some of the richest unmined ore on the planet.

He'd picked me up and brought me back to Nightside City and registered me in the city hospital under a false name, and he'd set up a credit account against his assets to pay my bills; then he'd called on 'Chan to see if he knew what the hell I had been doing that got me so close to getting killed.

'Chan didn't know anything, of course, but he was still interested in seeing me, seeing that I was all right. We still check on each other sometimes. Ever since Dad bought the dream and Mama shipped out, 'Chan and Ali and I had been all the family any of us had. We weren't really close —I think we're all afraid that if we get too close we'll just get burned again—but we stayed in touch, all three of us until Ali left, and then just 'Chan and me. So he came and took a look at me and then went back to his work. He was a croupier at the time—I'm not sure which casino, because he moved around, but it was obviously one of the better ones if it used human croupiers, right?

Anyway, Mishima had a lot of bucks invested in me, and it wasn't because he actually expected me to pay him back for the eye or anything else—he knew how broke I was. At least, he said he did, but I suspected he'd underestimated it a bit. In any case, he knew I couldn't reimburse him for anything. No, what he said he really wanted was just to know what the hell was going on. He said that was worth more to him than the money.

I could understand that. I wasn't sure I believed it of him, and I thought he might be gambling on buying a share of a lucrative bit of business, but I could understand his curiosity. Even so, even if it *was* just curiosity and there wasn't any admixture of greed, I still wasn't too sure I really wanted to tell him everything.

I said so.

I thought he'd be pissed at that, after he'd gone and told me that whole story, but he wasn't, or if he was he didn't show it. He was calm and reasonable instead.

"Look," he said. "You're in trouble, Hsing. Somebody tried to kill you. The only reason they didn't manage it is because I got myself involved. Whoever it was, and whatever you did to them, if they find out you're alive, they'll probably try again. And this time, if you don't tell me what's going on, I won't be there to help."

"I know that," I said. I tried not to sound defensive.

"Do you?" He pantomimed spitting in disgust—if he'd really spat the hospital would probably have thrown him out. "Look, I can tell people where you are and leave you to take care of yourself, or if you play along, I can keep my secrets to myself and even get you some guards. My treat—I won't put them on your bill."

"Generous of you," I said sarcastically.

He ignored that. "Look, you know, you've impressed me. When you caught that grithead at the Starshine it ticked me off, I admit—I thought you'd been lucky, cutting in ahead of me, and that you'd been poking in where you had no business. It didn't look ethical, where I was already on it. But it was a good piece of work. And you've been surviving out in the burbs on nothing for years, and that must be damn near impossible. And now you've latched onto something big and you can't handle it by yourself."

"Who says I can't handle it?" I snapped.

"*I* say so," he snapped right back. "The guy who found you frying on the dayside. Sure, you'd crawled halfway back, but you weren't going to make it, Hsing, and you know that as well as I do. You were dead if I hadn't found you."

He paused for a minute, staring at me, and then added, "Hell, most people would have been dead already. You're tough, I'll give you that. Your *symbiote* died, for chrissake! I've seen them pump healthy symbiotes out of miners dead for a week, but you walked yours to its death and you're still breathing! Damn!" He shook his head in apparent disbelief. Then he took a breath and went on. "You got me off the subject, though. What I was going to say was that I can see where you don't want to tell me everything and then let us go on separately. You'd be worried I'd be screwing you over, and I'd be worried about what you were doing, too. I don't want that. Instead I want to offer you a partnership on this case of yours, whatever it is—the two of us working it together, instead of competing. We split everything even, and we forget about the eye and the medical bills. Hell, if it works out maybe we can keep it going—Mishima and Hsing, Confidential Investigations. How's that sound?"

"Like a cheap vid entertainment," I said, but I didn't mean it. The truth is that it sounded pretty good. I was tired of trying to do everything on my own all the time, and as Big Jim's partner, I figured, I'd be able to work in the Trap again.

But then I remembered that unless Nakada's scheme worked, there wouldn't be any work in the Trap in a few years. There wouldn't be any *people* in the Trap. It would all be in daylight.

I'd had enough daylight to last me forever. I didn't need any more. I wanted the city to stay on the nightside. The only chance I had of getting that had nothing to do with Mishima; it was up to the Ipsy.

And I still didn't know why Lee and Orchid and Rigmus

had tried to kill me. And I didn't know whether Nakada's stunt had a chance of working.

And I didn't see any money in the case, no matter what happened. If I went any further with Mishima, I had to let him know that.

"Hey," I said. "I'll let you in on one secret, anyway. I'll tell you how much my fee is on this job that's nearly gotten me killed and cost you a few dozen kilobucks. Then you can tell me whether that partnership offer is still good, whether you want a piece of the action, or whether you'd rather just dump me back on the dayside."

"All right," he said, nodding. "I'll log on. What's the fee?"

"Two hundred and five credits. Flat fee, no expenses, no contingencies." I kept my face deadpan.

He stared for a minute, then slowly grinned at me. "Charity work, Hsing? For those squatters? Is that what all that crap about rent collectors was about?"

"You got it," I said.

"Squatters? God, Hsing, you almost got killed for a bunch of squatters?" The grin broadened.

"Hey," I said. "Out in the burbs I take what I can get." I grinned back.

His grin grew wider, and then he chuckled, and then he burst out laughing, leaning back, roaring with laughter, so that the chair had to struggle and squirm to keep him from falling.

I was glad to see that. I was pleased that he was taking it that way, as something to laugh at. After all, it was costing him one hell of a lot of money, for the eye and the rescue and the medical bills.

So I was glad he was laughing, instead of threatening to take it all out of me somehow.

For myself, I didn't laugh. Oh, I saw the humor in it, certainly, but I was a little too close to laugh at it. It wasn't just money for me; somebody had tried to kill me. I was lying there in a hospital, up to my bald little head in debt, and I could see the humor, but I wasn't ready to laugh at anything yet.

"Oh, Hsing," he said. "I'm going to enjoy working with you—if it doesn't bankrupt me!"

I grinned, then managed to laugh with him a little after all, and it was at least partly genuine.

Part of it was relief at Mishima's reaction. Part of it was something more.

I thought I would enjoy working with him, too. I'd worked alone long enough.

I might live longer with a backup.

Chapter Seventeen

WE LAUGHED AND BANTERED FOR A WHILE, BUT EVEN-
tually we got back to business. He still wanted to
know what the case was, and how the hell a two-hundred-
buck job had got me stranded on the dayside.

"Someone was trying to collect rent from all the squatters in the West End," I told him. "They wanted me to stop
it, keep them from being evicted."

"So?" he said. "That's a simple shakedown. You call the
cops, they take care of it. If they don't, you hire muscle.
Hsing, you aren't muscle. You're tough, I won't argue
that, but you're small, and up until now you worked alone.
Muscle can't work alone; a bullet or a needle can kill anybody. So why'd they come to you?"

"First off," I said, "they *did* call the cops, more or less.
They called the city, anyway. The rent collectors were
legit; they really were working for the new owners."

Mishima blinked at me. "*What* new owners?" he demanded. "Dawn's coming, Hsing; who'd be buying?"

"*That*," I said, "is what the squatters hired me to find

180

out. And no, they didn't try hiring muscle; they couldn't afford it. Not when the collectors looked legal. They might have had to take on the cops. Besides, I was a lot cheaper."

He stared at me for a moment. "All right," he said. "So that was the job? Find out who the new owners are?"

"Find out, and stop them from charging rents or evicting the squatters," I explained.

"All right, then," he said. "What did you find out?"

"I found out that somebody—one person, using fifteen names—had bought up most of the West End. Listen, Mishima, are you sure you want in on this?"

"Yeah, of course I'm sure," he said. "Who was it?"

"Don't be so sure, damn it," I told him. "Remember, this is the case that got me dumped on the dayside."

"I hadn't forgotten that, Hsing. I can take care of myself. Now, who the hell was it?"

I hated telling him. It was like giving up a piece of myself. I owed him, though, and I had to tell him.

"Sayuri Nakada," I said.

He blinked again. "No shit," he said, staring at me. "Nakada's buying the West End?"

I nodded.

"Why?" he asked.

I called to a service module in the back wall for a drink of water, which slid out on a floater. I sipped that down slowly before I answered.

"That's where it gets tricky," I said. "I found an answer, but it may not be right, and it gets messy from here on. I don't know everything I'd like to."

"Go on," he said.

I was past the worst part, giving up Nakada's name. The rest wasn't that much. "Nakada has hired a bunch of the brains—the human ones—at the Ipsy to stop Nightside City from crossing onto the dayside. She really thinks they can do it."

He considered that. "She does?" he asked.

"Yes, she does," I said.

"Can they?" he asked.

"I don't know," I said truthfully. "Probably not. I'll get to that."

He nodded. "Go on."

I went on. "Apparently, Paulie Orchid got her together with them—you know him?"

Mishima nodded again. "I've heard of him."

"I don't know whose idea it was originally, whether it was Nakada or Orchid or this person Lee at the Ipsy who came up with the whole thing. I hadn't gotten that far. I had talked to Nakada, and gotten the story from her, that the crew at the Ipsy was going to set off a fusion charge that would stop Epimetheus right where it is, before it rotated the city past the terminator. She'd have bought up as much of the city as possible, at cheap dawn's-coming prices, and would be running smooth after the bang, when dawn isn't coming anymore and land values head for high orbit. Simple enough, right?"

Mishima didn't answer. I went on. "Then I went over to the Ipsy to get some details, because the way Nakada told it, with just one big fusion charge, it not only wouldn't work, it *obviously* wouldn't work, so obviously that nobody but an idiot like Sayuri Nakada could take it seriously. If they tried it the way she described it, they'd probably wreck the whole city, and without even slowing down the sunrise. I figured Nakada had it wrong. But the people at the Ipsy wouldn't talk to me. I don't mean they took convincing, or that they were hostile; I mean they wouldn't talk, they wouldn't even tell me why they wouldn't talk. I mean, even when I waved a gun around and acted dangerous, they said nothing, absolutely nothing. So after I got tired of the silent treatment I threatened to put everything I knew on the nets, which I figured would crash their whole system, or at the very least cut Nakada's profits, but they were *still* not talking, which seemed crazy. Finally, I got an agreement that they'd talk it over and get back to me in two hours—but instead they horsed me with a neural interrupt, and Orchid and his buddy Bobo Rigmus paid me that little visit you saw." I shrugged. "And that's it."

Mishima considered that for a long minute. "Either I missed something, or that's just crazy," he said. "Why'd they try to kill you? Hell, why didn't they just tell you what you wanted to know? Didn't they try and buy you off first, or anything?"

"Nope." I shook my head emphatically. "Never offered me a buck."

"But that's haywire!"

"I know it is," I said.

Mishima sat back to think matters over. I lay back to let him. I was tired; I might be healed, but that didn't mean I was healthy. I was horribly aware of the absence of my symbiote; without it, I could catch diseases, I could be seriously injured in stupid little accidents, I'd take weeks to heal up if I damaged myself. And I didn't have much of a reserve of strength of my own anymore.

I closed my eyes and rested for a moment. Then Mishima cleared his throat, and I looked up at him again.

"So you blew my spy-eye down to keep me from seeing you talk to Nakada?" he asked.

I nodded. I hadn't mentioned that, but he was smart enough to work it out for himself. It didn't seem important.

"I don't know about that, Hsing. I mean, yeah, you were probably smart to try and keep me from finding out Nakada was involved, but shooting the eye just got me mad."

I shrugged. "I had a point to make. I don't take kindly to that sort of harassment."

"Yeah," he said slowly. "Yeah, I can see that. Okay. I still don't like it, but I see your point." He went on considering my story, and I rested a little more.

"So why were you after all the details of Nakada's little scheme?" he asked. "I mean, all that stuff at the Ipsy—what did that have to do with the squatters' rents?"

"Nothing," I said, opening my eyes. "But if somebody's going to wreck the city, I want to know about it." It struck me that he was worrying about all the wrong details. I'd gotten beyond worrying about the squatters; I was only concerned with whether Doc Lee and his buddies were going to crash the whole city.

"The city's doomed anyway," Mishima pointed out.

"Yeah," I said, getting a little annoyed. "But if I'm still here when they wreck it, I could get killed."

"True enough." He settled back to think some more.

I was doing a little thinking of my own, and I thought I had an idea. I was remembering some of what I'd been thinking back in my office when I got horsed, and again on the dayside. I thought I saw why they might have done what they did—the silent treatment and the attempted disappearance both. If I was right, it would be a relief in some ways, but a bit anticlimactic.

Mishima interrupted my chain of thought. "Hsing," he said. "It seems to me that you've got a big edge on them now. They tried to kill you. That's illegal."

The illegality of attempted murder was not exactly hot news to me, and I was not impressed. "So?" I said.

"So you can get Orchid and Rigmus put in for reconstruction. We've got your testimony, we've got my tapes from the sky-eye, and there's got to be other evidence. Charge them with attempted murder. I'll back you up."

"Yeah," I said. "But where does that get us? It may keep them from trying again, but I'm not even sure of that; I think it might be Doc Lee who's running the whole program. And while I can see how revenge might be fun, I hadn't figured *you'd* care about it. Are you developing a civic consciousness or something, trying to get criminals off the streets?"

"Hey, no, don't you see?" he said. "It gives you leverage. You've got a hold on them. Maybe you can pry what you want out of them with it."

I couldn't see using the attempted murder as a bargaining chip until I knew just what the hell was going on. Yes, it ought to work, but then, I had thought that threatening to put everything on the nets should have worked, too. "And maybe I can't," I said. "Or maybe I don't want to. Look, Mishima, I appreciate what you've done for me, and I can definitely see working for you—"

"*With* me," he interrupted, and I accepted the correction.

"With you, then. I can see that. But not on this case. We're going at it from different angles, and I can't work your way on it. It's too important. You seem to keep missing what I consider the real central issue here. You ask about the squatters, and you suggest getting Orchid and Rigmus put away, and ordinarily, that would be fine—you're protecting the client, concerned with my safety, and on most cases that would be great, but on this one my priorities are a little different. My first priority is the future of Nightside City. That's more important than squatters are, or than I am. If the city's destroyed, we're all dead anyway. Who cares about the rents in the West End if there's no West End?"

He considered that for a minute. "I see your point, I guess, but I'm not used to thinking in those terms. Just what is it you think these people are planning? I know you said something about a fusion charge, but I didn't follow that. When you said they might wreck the city, I thought you were talking about bankrupting it, or knocking down buildings after it's evacuated."

I shook my head. "No, that's not it at all. Nakada says that they intend to secretly rig and set off a fusion charge big enough to halt the planet's rotation, before the sun rises. Before the sun rises means no evacuation. That means there will still be people in the city. And a fusion charge big enough to do the job is enough to do one hell of a lot of damage if something goes wrong, and I don't see how a scheme that simple could go *right*. Look, if there were any economically sound way of saving the city, don't you think the casinos would be trying it? They've talked about it for years now, but they've never come up with anything. You think Sayuri Nakada and Paulie Orchid are smarter than the best the casinos can do?"

"The casinos weren't figuring on buying the whole city up cheap beforehand," he pointed out.

"Doesn't matter," I said. "If it can make Nakada rich, it could have let a consortium break even, at the very least."

He didn't argue with that. "So what do you think is happening? Is this all just a front, and they tried to kill you before you found out what's *really* going on?"

I nodded. He'd hit my little idea pretty squarely— maybe it was obvious, and I'd been too close to the case to see it before. "I think that just might be it, yeah. But you're getting off the track again. It's the city I'm worried about."

"Go on," he said.

"Look," I said. "Just because the fusion charge can't work, just because it's probably going to leave the whole city flat as that desert you found me on, that doesn't mean these people aren't going to try it, and try it while there are still people here. Or even if they do wait until the city's been evacuated, there are still going to be miners scattered all over the nightside who could get killed." I didn't mention the possibility of a meltdown. That seemed too damn melodramatic; I didn't think Mishima was the kind of person who thought in those terms. He'd just about said he wasn't.

That didn't mean I thought a meltdown was impossible; it just meant I didn't think Mishima would take it seriously.

Overkill from a botched fusion charge, though,—*that* he could accept.

"Yeah," he said. "I see that."

I nodded. "So, I have *got* to find out what they're really doing. And if they're really going to flatten the city, I've got to stop them. That's more important than anything."

"I see that, too," he said.

I waited, and he went on. "Hsing, you were right. I'm out of my depth here. I came in in the middle, and I don't know a damn thing about all this fusion-charge stuff. You handle it, you do it all your way, and I'll back you up. You need muscle, I've got three good people on retainer. You need com service, I've got some nice stuff. You need an in anywhere, I'll see what I can do. You just keep me updated, and I won't interfere. And when it's done, we're partners, all right?"

"Either that," I said, "or you can try and collect what I owe you from my estate."

I was joking, but I was also puzzled. Did Mishima really think I was that valuable? Why was he going along with all this? Why was he so eager to take me on as a partner?

But as I'd just told him, Nightside City was the important thing. I would worry about just what the Ipsy was really planning for the city, and when that was settled I could try and figure out Big Jim's program. Once I knew whether the city was about to be reduced to radioactive debris or not I could worry about loose ends like Orchid and Rigmus.

I was tired of talk. I was ready to get back to work.

Chapter Eighteen

THE HOSPITAL LET ME GO WITHOUT AN ARGUMENT, AND I got a cab home. I'd borrowed a couple of hundred credits from Mishima to make sure my card would keep working. That put me a notch deeper into the hole, but I couldn't see any way around it.

My Sony-Remington was still lying on my desk where Orchid had dropped it, and the holster was somewhere on the dayside; I got an old shoulderbag and put the gun in that. Then I sat down at my desk and got the com up and running.

The first step was to kick all my security into high, and to hell with the cost. The next step was worse.

I stopped for a minute to fight down trembling before I plugged myself back in, but I knew I'd need to run on wire for what I had to do next, so I held myself still and jacked in. I wasn't expecting any more horses. I just had to hope that Mishima was playing straight, and that he'd sent the protection he'd promised. The high eye was back overhead, another normal-field spy-eye was on its way, and tracer microintelligences were all over the area—but not on me, because without a symbiote the damn things might kill me if I picked up enough to clog an artery. The hospital had given me a little anti-invasive treatment that was supposed to last a week or so—one more item on the bill Mishima was paying—but I was still eagerly avoiding micros of any description as much as I could. It could have been my mind playing tricks, but I had a constant reminder of my unprotected status—I itched, and I hadn't really itched since I was a little girl. Even the cheap symbiote I'd had had taken care of itches.

I didn't let that distract me. I knew what I was after. Money leaves a trail. If the people at the Ipsy were working for Nakada, she had to be paying them. I wanted to know where that money was going and what they were buying with it. I had a theory I wanted to check out.

If they were planting fusion charges, they had to be buying them, or buying materials for them, or at the very least buying the building programs for their microassemblers. If they were planning anything at all, they'd have expenses of some sort. I intended to take a look at those expenses.

I wasn't expecting trouble. After all, Lee's bunch thought I was dead—or at least they were supposed to think that. They shouldn't have been on guard.

They weren't. I got back to that numbered account, the one Nakada had used for her real estate purchases, without any problems at all. Getting a list of all outgoing payments wasn't too difficult, either.

Besides that one, I tracked down and checked out every other account Nakada had used for her real estate buys. I went back to my old list of property transactions and traced every one of them back to Nakada—sometimes directly, sometimes through blinds, sometimes through Orchid—and then I traced forward on every account.

Just as I figured, she'd paid one hell of a lot of money to Paulie Orchid. I couldn't find anything directed to Lee or Rigmus or anyone else at the Ipsy, but there was plenty that had gone to Orchid, and I set out to trace that.

That was easier than I had any right to expect. Orchid was an idiot. He had no security at all on any of his accounts, and he generally used his right name.

Once the money came in, it went nine ways. A little of each deposit got shunted off to a numbered account; I figured that was either expense money, or Orchid skimming a little before his friends got their fingers into the pot. The rest got divided into eight even shares.

One share went off-planet, as negotiable securities on every ship outbound for Prometheus. My guess was that that was Orchid's own cut, being tucked away safely out of sight.

Another share went to an account for Beauregard Rigmus, at Epimethean Commerce.

Another went to Mahendra Dhuc Lee.

The others went to five other people at the Ipsy, all human.

I noted all their names and numbers, and then I dropped that line for the time being and went at the Ipsy's financial records.

What I was after was simple enough. I wanted information on everything that the Ipsy, or anyone working there, had bought lately, or had delivered anywhere, with special attention paid to Doc Lee and the five others on my list.

I wanted to see if they were really assembling a monster fusion charge, or some huge tractor to pull the crater westward, or any other device that might have a shot at saving the city.

I'll save you all the details. It took me six hours, and you don't want to hear it all, so I'll just tell you what I found.

They weren't.

All the money from Sayuri Nakada was going straight into personal accounts, and then being sent on to more personal accounts on Prometheus, and it was staying there. No money from the Ipsy's regular accounts was going into fusion charges or any other sort of heavy equipment that might conceivably be used to stop a planet's rotation or move an entire city. In fact, no money from the Ipsy was going anywhere; except for my six little darlings, the Institute was effectively shut down and bankrupt. Its funding had dried up about two years back, when its best people had decided to beat the rush and emigrate.

My guess was right. The city was safe from any glitching rescue attempts. The whole thing was a fraud, a scam, a way to pry enough money out of Nakada for those eight people to get off Epimetheus and live comfortably on Prometheus.

Except, of course, the city was still going to fry on schedule. That was why these eight wanted off.

I unplugged myself and stared at the screen for a moment, at the list of the eight names. Then I leaned back, touching keys without thinking about it, and watched as the big holo across the room lit up with a scene of robot beasts in spikes and armor churning up an alien landscape and each other in some sort of competition.

I was at the bottom of the puzzle, I was pretty sure. I had it all. And I was disappointed.

It was all a cheap little swindle. Nightside City would not get a last-minute reprieve.

It wouldn't go out in a sudden blaze of glory, taking the entire planet with it, either. It would slowly cook away and wind up an empty ruin out on the dayside, just the way we'd all thought it would all along.

It was often that way, in my line of work. The big cases don't turn out as big as you think they will. Sordid little details don't lead to criminal masterminds, or big breaks in vast schemes—they just lead to more sordid little details.

These eight people, desperate to get off-planet without winding up broke, had put together a con and picked Sayuri Nakada as their mark. They had tried to kill me when I came looking at it, not because they were afraid I'd tell the cops, or ruin Nakada's profits, but because they didn't want me to uncover the fraud and tell Nakada she was being swindled.

And that was all there was to it.

Except that their little scheme had started affecting other people. The squatters were going to be evicted. The real estate market in the city was probably going to be all screwed up. Sayuri Nakada was probably running on family credit, and when the plot failed and the sun rose she might drag the entire Nakada family down with her—at least, I thought so for a minute or two, but then I changed my mind. The Nakadas wouldn't be stupid enough to let Sayuri get at that much money. They could lose a few hundred megabucks and never notice it.

All that was from the con, but the con wasn't all these people had done. They had tried to kill me. What's more, they had cost Mishima a good chunk of money, in the expenses he'd paid for me. I felt I owed him that money, so they hadn't just tried to kill me, they'd driven me a long way into debt.

I *hate* being in debt!

They owed me for this.

I still had a client, too, and that meant I still had work to do.

They owed me, and they were going to pay.

I wanted to start with Sayuri Nakada. She was the one with the money, after all, the one who was stupid enough to fall for the scheme. I wanted to start with her, but I didn't. After a little thought I decided to save her for later.

I was going to start with Paulie Orchid. Unless I was bending data, he was the one who had put it all together. The fact that he was the one doling out the money proved that. He'd needed some scientists to shill for him, so he'd found Doc Lee and his team at the Ipsy, all of them desperate for money; that wouldn't have been beyond even Orchid's talents. The idea of Rigmus or Lee organizing the plot just didn't fit; it had to be Orchid.

So he was the mastermind, and he was also the one who had tried to kill me. He was the most dangerous of the whole array. I'd underestimated him when I thought he was nothing but a bit of gritware; he was stupid in a lot of ways, but not in every way. He was too stupid to put any security on his bank accounts, but he'd been smart enough to play a pretty damn good con. He'd dropped out of sight for a long time before he'd come up with this scheme; maybe he'd had some modification done, and I don't just mean the wire job. You can buy just about any sort of add-on you want, for either brain or body, and he might have bought anything. I didn't know just what he was capable of, and I wanted to have surprise on my side when I went after him.

So Orchid came first.

I called Mishima at his office. He was cheerful, giving me the whole routine about being glad to hear from me.

I wasn't in the mood to chat. I cut through the banter and told him I wanted the muscle he'd offered me. I didn't tell him anything about con games, didn't give him any names; I just said I was going to pay Orchid a visit and needed some backup. Armed backup.

He dropped the friendship display. He nodded and agreed, and we broke the connection.

I called a cab, and half an hour later I met the muscle Mishima had sent me on the street at the entrance to Orchid's apartment tower—three of them, all big. Any one of them must have weighed over twice what I did, and they all wore slick armor, the transparent tight-bond monomolecular stuff. The woman had retractable claws. The bigger, darker man had fangs that gleamed as bright as the wires in his face. The smaller man was heavily cyborged, half his face rebuilt with chrome. Serious muscle. You don't go in for the surgical stuff for fun.

Maybe the cyborg had gone into it because he had to be rebuilt anyway, but the other two, they'd done it just for business.

They were all armed with light little pieces, street-legal in the city.

They were perfect.

Using a voice distorter and no image, I called up to Orchid's apartment, saying I was collecting contributions for a campaign to outlaw gambling on Epimetheus. Rigmus answered.

I gave him my story, and he told me to eat wire and die. I was polite; I asked if anyone else was around who might be more generous.

He offered to feed the wire up my ass personally.

I asked if there was anyone else there I could talk to, more generous or not, and said I'd been told Paulie Orchid lived there. I made it sound like Orchid had been sold to me as the savior of the downtrodden.

Yeah, Rigmus told me, Orchid was in, but he was busy, and of course he wasn't interested.

I just needed to know he was there. I shut up and exited the call.

The four of us went up the tower together, the muscle and me, and I stood back with my gun in my hand while the cyborg took out the door security.

But the cyborg wasn't the first one in. The instant the door opened I was through and into the room.

It was a big apartment, and a good address, but those

two hadn't done it justice. The place was all done in maroon and red, with flat golden walls and no holos anywhere except a cheap vidset hanging in one corner. The furniture was strictly inert—no color shifts, legs holding everything up—and there wasn't much of it. What there was didn't look new, either. I figured Orchid and Rigmus had blown away all the juice they could spare in getting the place, with nothing left to furnish it decently.

Or maybe they figured it wasn't worth the trouble, since it was temporary. They were both bound for Prometheus when their little scam had played out.

The best piece there was a big maroon sofa, pushed back hard against one wall. Rigmus was sitting on it, holding a jackbox.

I dove for him. He dropped the jackbox and dodged, leaning awkwardly sideways, and I twisted around and took him in the throat with the side of the hand holding the gun.

He grunted and then grabbed for me. I think he figured he'd just break me in half, small as I am.

I don't break that easy.

I got him under the jaw, bent his head back, and rammed it against the wall. Hard.

He got an arm around my waist and tried to pull me away, and I rammed his head back against the wall again, then drove the butt of the HG-2 into his larynx. I felt something give. His stomach growled, which seemed weirdly inappropriate, and I wondered whether it had anything to do with my blow.

The cyborg was coming up behind me, but I waved him back. This was personal. Rigmus had tried to kill me.

He was flailing about, not connecting. I put a finger into his left eye and pressed down.

He was lucky my fingernails hadn't really grown back yet.

He tried to scream, but he couldn't because of what I'd done to his throat and because I was stuffing a hand into his mouth, choking him with my fist.

He didn't even have the wits to try and bite me, and I just pounded his head back against the wall until he collapsed.

I'll tell you, it was pretty damn satisfying to finally be able to do something that simple and direct and to have it *work*. I have some pretty serious moral reservations about using any more violence than necessary—but I forget them sometimes. I shouldn't, but I do.

When he slumped I got off him and let him fall. He landed sprawled across a corner of the couch, which managed to reshape itself enough to keep him from falling to the floor.

He lay there, less than half conscious, and his stomach growled again. I almost laughed.

The female muscle took over with him, sitting on him with a claw at his throat, while the cyborg opened the bedroom doors.

The first bedroom was empty, just a white bed floating in the center unmade and a wardrobe dispenser in one corner—nothing else.

Orchid was in the second. This one was done in red and gold, and any juice he'd saved on the rest of the place he'd blown here. The walls were holos, running erotic vids on all four sides, but I didn't let the movement distract me. I knew holos from real, and I knew Orchid when I saw him.

He was on the bed, with a woman and his pants down, and a privacy field up so he hadn't heard us coming. I ran in and grabbed him before he saw us.

He was too surprised to resist. I shoved him over onto the floor, and when he opened his mouth to protest I stuck the muzzle of the HG-2 in it and flicked the power switch.

I felt the gun tick to life. Orchid saw the pilot light glow red, then green.

The woman started to scream, but Mishima's muscle pulled her off, and one of them, the one with the fangs, held her quiet in the corner while I negotiated with Mis' Orchid. He let her straighten her outfit, a mess of frills and drifting colors that could have hidden almost anything, but he kept his gun at her throat.

The cyborg took the apartment door for his post, first watching out, then watching in, in quick, steady alternation; good, solid work.

"Now, Mis' Paul Orchid," I said. "We have a few things to get straight."

He didn't say anything. He couldn't, with the gun where it was. His eyes widened a little, though, and I think it was only then, when he heard my voice, that he recognized me. I looked pretty different with just a thin fuzz on the top of my head, instead of real hair, and with hardly any eyebrows.

Besides, he'd thought I was dead.

"First off," I said, "I know why you tried to kill me. I know all about the scam you're running on Sayuri Nakada. I know you wanted to keep me from telling her it was a con. But you screwed up, grithead. It wasn't any of my business; I don't owe Nakada anything. If you hadn't tried to kill me, you fucking idiot, I wouldn't have cared, but you—you made it my business by dumping me on the dayside. That makes it very personal." I shifted the gun, so he could hear the mechanism working as it compensated for my movement. An HG-2 hasn't got room for sound-proofing, which was fine with me—it added a bit to the effect.

He made a noise, but I wasn't finished.

"Now, you may be recording this. You may think you've got me on charges of trespassing, and assault, and terroristic threatening. You may even be right. But, you stupid son of a bitch, *I've* got *you* for kidnapping and attempted murder even if I *don't* give Nakada the code on your program. Did you really think I was so dumb I didn't have *any* security you didn't bypass? I have full-spectrum authentic vid of you and Bobo carting me out to the cab and sending me east over the crater wall. I have witnesses. I won't even mention that I have all the evidence I need in my head and in the cab itself. And it's all on record in a dozen places where you can't get at it."

He made a sort of a squeak. I rammed the gun against his teeth. "Now," I said, "if we've got it all very clear as to what the basis for negotiation is—which is, that I'm in charge, I know what's going on, and I've got you a hell of a lot tighter than you've got me—then I can let you up and we can talk business. What do you say?"

He squeaked again and tried to nod.

I had been kneeling on top of him, my face centimeters from his; now I backed off and got up.

"One more thing," I said, while he was picking himself up and fastening his pants. "If we do wind up pressing charges against each other, I want you to know that I didn't like the dayside at all, and I do hold grudges. I'm big on revenge. If you go to trial and they convict—and by god they should, with what I've got on record—then I've got my victim's privilege coming, and I have it all picked out. I had time to think about it out there in the sun, plenty of time. I want your balls cut off, permanently and without anesthetic. Drastic, I know, but for kidnapping and attempted murder I think I could get it. You just keep that in mind while we talk, okay?"

Actually, I didn't really think I'd ask for that, but it made one hell of a good threat for someone like Orchid.

He nodded, rubbing his jaw.

He thought I had more to say, but I waited. It was his turn.

"All right, Hsing, what do you want?" he asked at last.

"It's about time, damn it, that you bothered to ask me that before you started giving me trouble. It's simple enough. But I'm going to keep you in suspense until you answer a question for me. Just who did you think hired me?"

He stared, then blinked. Those fancy eyes of his looked stupid when they blinked. "Ah . . ." he said. "I thought the New York . . ."

He let it trail off.

I'd been expecting something like that, but I still couldn't really believe it. The adrenaline I'd built up in tackling Rigmus got to me, with no symbiote to cut it back, and I lost control. I shoved the gun under his nose. "You *stupid*, worthless piece of shit!" I screamed at him. "You coprophagous cretin! The New York wouldn't touch me with a goddamn run of scrubware! Don't you know anything? Are you too dumb to ask anyone a simple question? I can't get work in the Trap. I haven't been able to for years!"

He stammered something, but I wasn't listening. He was backed against the bed, his knees starting to buckle as my gun forced him back.

"I wasn't investigating you, or Nakada, or the Ipsy—I was hired to find out why somebody was trying to collect rent in the West End! I was hired by a bunch of *squatters*, you poor fool! That's all! You could swindle Nakada out of her liver, and I wouldn't have cared, if you hadn't hassled the squatters out there! You . . . you . . ."

I ran out of words and felt my finger tightening on the trigger; I forced it to loosen, forced myself to calm down. I stepped back and lowered the gun, and then I took a deep breath.

He sat down on the bed. "So what do you want?" he asked, his voice unsteady.

"It's simple," I told him. "I want you to stop hassling me. I want you to stop hassling the squatters, even if it means you have to pay Nakada's rents out of your share of the take from your scam. I want guarantees on both of those, recorded with the city and with the cops—we can word it so we don't have to incriminate anybody. I want it understood that if you ever come near me again I'm going to use this gun, without warning, and plead self-defense with those kidnapping records to back me up. I want all of that from both you and Rigmus, and if you can get it, from Doc Lee and the others at the Ipsy. If you can't get it from them, tell me, and I'll go talk it over with them. I know your scheme to stop the city is phony, and you can tell them that I know, and I can prove it. I don't want them trying any stupid demonstrations for Nakada—if you can't string her any farther just with words, then take your money and exit, don't try and push your luck, or I'll see that you regret it. And I want you to know that if you try to kill me again, even if you succeed, you're dead meat. I'm not stupid enough to make a play like this without backup, not when you've taken one shot at me already. These three aren't the only friends I've got. You got all that?"

He nodded. "I've got it."

"Any problem with any of it?"

"No," he said, and he shook his head. "No problem."

I smiled. "There!" I said. "That wasn't so bad, was it? There *is* one more little detail, but we'll get to that in a minute. First I want to see you make those guarantees I mentioned." I pointed toward a nearby screen and jack. "Go to it."

He did. I think I'd made an impression; he didn't try anything at all, did it all up properly. The contracts didn't mention reasons—they just stated that Paul Orchid undertook to remove himself and any agents in his employ from all self-initiated contact with Carlisle Hsing and with all persons resident within a half-kilometer radius of the intersection of Western and Wall. Breach of contract would be punishable to the fullest extent of the law—and in Nightside City, with its casino-based economy, that was plenty.

The muscle with the claws dragged Rigmus in, more or less conscious, jacked him in, and had him thumb his copies of the same agreements.

Then Orchid called the Ipsy and relayed my messages to Doc Lee. "She means it," he told them.

And I did mean it, every word of it, except the bit about the victim's privilege.

Lee seemed shaken, but he swallowed and smiled and agreed, then put it on record over the com. Each of the five others then took a turn doing the same. Nobody gave me any back talk this time.

When that was taken care of I said, "All right, Orchid, just one more detail, and you and your woman can get back to what you were doing, if I haven't spoiled the mood."

The woman made a noise, but I ignored it. This wasn't her business. The muscle with fangs still had his gun at her throat, and that was fine with me. I didn't know anything about her; for all I knew, if he hadn't had the gun there, she might have jumped me. Of course, attacking me would have been stupid, but I had serious doubts about the good sense of anyone I found in bed with Paulie Orchid—particularly someone dressed like that. Her outfit was mostly greens, which went nicely with her skin but clashed with the room she was in, and it floated off in various directions, giving fleeting glimpses of bare flesh—not exactly your practical garment.

"All right, Hsing," Orchid said, resigned. "What is it? What's the detail?"

"Set me up a date with Sayuri Nakada," I said. "I want to talk to her."

He gaped at me, but he didn't have much choice. He made the call.

Chapter Nineteen

I DON'T KNOW WHY I WANTED TO SEE NAKADA IN PER-
son, but I did. It was important to me, somehow.

We met on neutral ground. We met at a little breakfast
bar on Second, in the middle of Trap Over. I was sitting
there waiting, with Mishima's muscle quiet in the background, when Nakada walked in with a piece of muscle of
her own and an entourage of floaters.

She didn't recognize me until I called her name.

"Mis' Nakada! Over here!"

She came and looked down at me. "What the hell happened to your hair?"

"Long story," I said. "You wouldn't be interested."

She shrugged and sat down.

I pointed at her muscle, a big guy with sleek, hairless
black skin that might or might not have been armored. If it
was armored, it was a better job than Mishima's bunch
could afford. "Do we need him?" I asked.

She glanced back at him, then waved him away. He
went to wait outside—there wasn't room in the bar.

Most of the floaters went with him; one stayed, a little golden multipurpose job, and I decided not to argue about it. After all, even if it left, Nakada still had implants down to the marrow, and I couldn't make her leave those outside.

The bar delivered my tea and puffcake, and I asked if she wanted anything. She shook her head.

"All I want," she said, "is to know why you got me down here."

I didn't answer directly. "How's the project going?" I asked.

She scowled at me. "The project?" she asked.

"Yeah," I said. "You know, the one that's going to make you rich."

She didn't like my manners, that was obvious, but she answered. "Bad," she said. "They hit some kind of snag in the mapping data. Everything's been delayed."

I nodded sympathetically. "Too bad," I said. "Remember your promise that you'd let me know when the date's set."

"I remember," she said.

I was playing this by guess, plugging in values as I went. I wasn't sure at all what I was doing, why I was there, or why Nakada was there. I just knew that I had to talk to her, and here I was, talking to her.

The obvious question was whether I should tell her that she was being rooked. The obvious answer was yes; I mean, why the hell not? I didn't owe Orchid and Lee anything.

And I wasn't sure it would make any difference. Hell, there was a good chance the whole scam was about to fall apart anyway. My own opinion was that if Orchid was running smooth he'd clear out, take what he'd gotten so far, and get off-planet without trying to bleed any more juice out of anyone.

I decided to try the direct and honest approach. "Mis'

Nakada, have you ever really looked at the scheme the Ipsy's selling you?"

She looked at me. "What do you mean?"

"I mean, doesn't it sound too good to be true? Have you checked it over to see whether it would really work? Have you discussed it with anyone, run their claims through any analytical software?"

She stared at me. "I don't understand what you're getting at."

"I'm getting at the question of whether Doc Lee and his bunch can actually do what they say they can," I said.

She almost snarled. "Of course they can," she said. "Lee's a top planetologist. His team's all top experts."

"Experts can lie, Mis' Nakada," I said.

"What do you mean?" she said.

"I mean that it's all a trick, a sham," I told her. "They can't stop the city, any more than anyone else can. They're conning you. They're just taking your money and tucking it away on Prometheus. You don't have to believe me; get any planetologist you like to come and take a look, and you'll see. They're swindling you."

She glared at me with a look that was about the closest I've ever seen to pure hatred. "You're lying. You're the one trying to con me."

"No, I'm not," I said. "I'm telling the truth."

"You're lying," she insisted. "Why would they cheat me?"

"For the money, of course," I told her.

"No," she said. "You're lying, that's all." Then she looked as if a brilliant idea occurred to her. "Did somebody hire you to get them away from me?" she demanded. "To get them to work for someone else?"

"No," I said. "Nobody hired me."

"*Somebody* did," she said. "Somebody's trying to stop me."

"Think what you like," I said, amazed at her ability to deny reality when it clashed with her desires.

I'd tried. I'd tried honesty, tried telling her what was happening. If she didn't accept it, it wasn't my fault. I'd done my full duty to truth and justice. Sayuri Nakada deserved to be swindled if anyone ever did; I could almost sympathize with Orchid, seeing all that money in the hands of someone like her.

Of course, if she checked up later and cut Orchid and Lee and the rest off, or got them sent up for reconstruction, I wouldn't weep.

Right now, though, I had one more thing I realized I had to discuss with her, and maybe it was something I should have dealt with before I antagonized her. I had a client to take care of. Just because Paulie and Bobo weren't going to be making the rounds in the West End didn't mean nobody would.

"There's one other thing," I said, casually. "I probably should have mentioned it the first time, but you know how it is, things can slip your mind."

She just glared. Maybe she didn't know how it is, with all the implants she must have had keeping her up to date. Or maybe she just didn't want to admit she knew.

"There's a little matter of some people I know," I said. "Living out in the West End in some of the buildings you bought."

"Squatters," she said.

I nodded. "You could call them that," I agreed.

"Burakumin!" she spat. "Abid! A bunch of social gritware. They pay rent or they get out; I don't want them around when I start cleaning up out there."

I held up a hand. "Mis' Nakada," I said, "I think you're overreacting. They aren't such bad people."

I was lying; they were scum. But they were also paying clients.

"What are they to you?" she asked.

"Friends," I lied. "And I don't want them evicted."

"*I* do," she said, and she was pretty damn definite about it. I guessed right then that collecting rents hadn't been Orchid's idea at all, but hers. I doubted Orchid had known just how much trouble collecting that stupid rent would buy him, but at least he hadn't come up with it on his own.

"Mis' Nakada," I said, "I hope you'll reconsider."

"Why should I?" she demanded.

"Because if you don't, I'll put everything I know about the little plan you have the Ipsy working on on the public nets. That could cut into your profits pretty badly, having the word get out too soon."

"That's blackmail," she said.

I shrugged. "You could call it that, I suppose," I admitted. "I have a chunk of information; I can hand it out free, or I can sell you the dissemination rights. If you want to call that blackmail, suit yourself. Which do you want? Do I put it on the nets or not?"

"No!" she said, sharp and hard.

"Then we make a deal," I said. "We can put it in writing. I'm not looking for anything permanent, just a little time for my friends to get relocated. I'll agree not to release to the public or anyone except partners or immediate family any information I may have concerning your investment plans or dealings with nonprofit scientific organizations, and I'll bind all partners and immediate family to the same commitment. In exchange, you'll agree that you will not attempt to collect any rents on property in the West End for, shall we say, three years?"

"That's too long," she snapped.

"All right," I said. "Until you're ready to refurbish the buildings, or three years, whichever comes first. The day your repair crews arrive, the squatters will be out; how's that sound?"

"How do I know you won't make more demands?" she asked.

"That's in my end of the agreement," I said. "If I spread the word, or if I demand anything more, then I'm in breach of contract—and you and I both know what the penalties are for that in Nightside City. I'm not interested in a term of indenture, or in selling body parts."

She thought for a minute, then nodded. "All right," she said.

That little golden floater had all the necessary equipment for the contract, and in fifteen minutes we had shaken hands and left.

I don't know where she went. I went home to my office. I thanked Mishima's muscle and let them fend for themselves; I didn't see that I needed them anymore.

The case was over, as far as I could see. I sat at my desk and ran through the records, making notes, seeing if I'd missed anything. I didn't see that I had. My contract was to stop the new owner from evicting the squatters; I had Nakada's agreement recorded and sealed. Side issues had been to find out who was doing what, and why, and I had all that figured out. Orchid and Rigmus had tried to kill me, but I had it set so they wouldn't try again.

It looked smooth. I started clearing everything out of the com's active memory.

Then the com beeped and I touched keys, and Mishima's face appeared.

"Hello, Hsing," he said.

"Hello, Mishima," I replied.

"So how'd it go?" he asked.

"How did *what* go?" I said.

"Your little talk with Sayuri Nakada—how'd it go?"

I wasn't terribly happy to hear him ask that. I was beginning to have second or third thoughts about any sort of partnership with Mishima. I'd always worked alone, my own way and at my own speed; having a partner checking up on me did not carry a lot of appeal. It had seemed wonderful when I was lying in a hospital bed with new eyes and my new skin still baby-slick, feeling vulnerable, with no idea how I could face down Orchid and the others all by myself, but now I began to see drawbacks.

I still appreciated the loan of the muscle, not to mention the medical bills and the detail that Mishima had ventured out onto the dayside to rescue me, and I could see virtues in the arrangement, but I didn't like being called to account like that.

"It went all right," I said, trying to think how I could put my concerns.

"What did you get?" he asked.

"What do you mean, what did I get?" I said.

"I mean, what did you get from Nakada?" he said. "How much did she pay you to keep quiet?"

"She didn't pay me anything," I said. "She just agreed to leave the squatters alone."

He stared at me for a minute. "Listen, partner," he said. "I don't want to get this relationship off to a rough start. Let's just keep the bugs and glitches to a minimum. Let's not hold out on each other, okay?"

"Sure," I said. "I'm not holding out."

"Oh, get off it, Hsing," he said. "You went there with all the details of this scam, with everything you needed to prove to Sayuri Nakada's old man back on Prometheus that she's a complete idiot, and you came away without a buck? You expect me to believe that?"

It was my turn to sit back and stare for a minute.

"All right, Mishima," I said. "Suppose you tell me how *you* think it ran."

He gave me a look like I'd just offered to buy his first-born child at an offensively low price.

"All right," he said. "I think you went in there and told

Nakada that she was being taken, that Orchid and Rigmus and Lee were running a scam on her that had made her look like a complete fool. I think she probably suspected it all along—I mean, the whole thing is so obviously too good to be true. I think you mentioned that her great-grandfather might be interested in knowing what she'd been doing with her money. I think you suggested that you might tell him, if the circumstances arose. I think she took the hint and asked what it would cost to be sure the circumstances never arose, and I think that the two of you dickered out a specific amount. Since she was a pro once, I suppose it wasn't all that much, but half of it's mine, Hsing. Now, how much was it?"

I shook my head. "You've got it wrong, Mishima. Right from the start."

"Then *you* tell *me* how it went," he demanded.

"You tell me something first," I said. "How'd you know it was all a scam?"

He paused, and I could see he was thinking back and realizing that I'd never told him that. He could say he figured it out for himself, but he was awfully damn sure that *I* knew it was a scam.

I guess he decided on the truth.

"I tapped into your com," he said.

"Hey, partner," I said. "Wasn't *that* a sweet thing to do! Hey, what rare trust between partners we have here!"

"Come on, Hsing," he said. "You were busy. We're partners. You owe me. I just saved us some time and argument."

"I'll tell you, Mishima," I said. "I don't think the team of Mishima and Hsing is going to make it. Sorry about that."

"Oh, come on," he said. "Give me a break!"

"I will," I said. "Don't worry. I know what I owe you. I just don't think that this partnership will run. I'm not going to screw you over if I can help it, Mishima, but I don't think I can work with you, either. I'm telling you that right now, up front."

"Hell," he said. "Just forget the partnership, then. I don't need you. But you owe me, Hsing, so tell me what you got from Nakada."

"I did tell you," I said. "Hey, how is it you didn't manage to listen in at the breakfast bar? Then we wouldn't be arguing about it."

I was being sarcastic, but Mishima took me seriously. "Nakada had privacy fields up," he said. "Those floaters of hers were loaded. I couldn't get anything through. And those three gritheads I loaned you didn't bother to try and hear; they figured I'd get it all from the machines. Even Jerzy."

"That the one with the chrome face?" I asked.

He nodded.

"You know," I said, "maybe they heard and just didn't want to tell you, figured it wasn't your business."

He spat, offscreen. "Don't give me that," he said. "Of course it's my business, and those three work for me. They didn't hear. You did."

"Right," I said. "And I told you what I got."

"So tell me again, and maybe add a few details," he said.

I nodded. "I'll do that," I said. "First off, you started off well with your little guessing game. I did tell Nakada the scheme was a fake. But you got her reaction wrong. She didn't believe me. Didn't believe a word, thought that *I* was the one running a con on her, trying to cut her out of the deal. They've got her clipped down tight."

"Oh, come on," he said. "Don't give me that shit."

"True," I said. "I swear it. Put it on wire, on oath, on stress-triggered plague test, I tell you she did not believe me."

"Hsing, *nobody* is that dumb!" he insisted.

"You ever *met* Nakada?" I asked. "She isn't exactly *dumb*, but she only believes what suits her. Stopping the sunrise suits her right down the line, and she wasn't taking any argument, so I didn't argue."

"That's *crazy*," he insisted.

I just shrugged.

It wasn't all that crazy, but he couldn't see it. He was Epimethean, like me—except maybe without as much imagination. I could dream about stopping the dawn, but to him, the sunrise was inevitable. He'd lived with it all his life. The idea of stopping it was just gibberish, like turning off gravity. He didn't realize that Nakada looked at it differently. To her, cities were permanent things, and the idea that this one was going to fold up and die, and that there was no way to stop it, was anathema.

The truth lay somewhere in between, I was pretty sure. With time and money and competent people, Nightside City could probably be saved—but it wasn't worth what it would cost. It would be one of the biggest engineering projects of all time, up there with the terraforming of Venus, but with only a city for payoff instead of an entire planet. A bad investment—but not unthinkable.

"You believe what you want," I said, "but Nakada doesn't think it's a scam. She still doesn't want the word spread, though, so we drew up a little agreement—I keep quiet, and she leaves the squatters alone. That's all. That's all I asked for."

He went back to that disbelieving stare.

"Hsing," he said, "I think I believe you. But if it's true, I've got to ask what the hell is *wrong* with you, passing up a chance like that!"

"I don't work that way." Then I exited the call.

I half expected him to call back, but he didn't, so I didn't have to explain it any further.

It was all clear to me, plain and simple. I'm a detective. I was then; I am now. I find things out. I sell people information. I keep quiet when I'm paid to.

But I'm not a blackmailer. Nakada hadn't hired me to find out anything, so she couldn't pay me to keep it quiet.

I'd stolen that information from her, because I needed it for my client. Information isn't like most property—you can steal it from someone without them ever knowing it's gone, and without depriving them of it. There's no law of conservation of information. You can multiply it from nothing to infinity.

But it was still Nakada's information. I had no right to spread it any further than I had to. If I took money from her to shut me up, I'd be stealing it.

And yeah, this is all hypocritical as hell. I *did* blackmail her, when I made her leave the squatters there. I'm not above selling information that isn't mine. I'm not above a little quiet blackmail. I do what I need to survive.

But I try and keep my self-respect. I try to stay inside my own limits. They aren't the limits the law sets, but they're limits. Sayuri Nakada had enough problems, what with her blind belief in the gritware Orchid and Lee were peddling her. I couldn't see taking her for all she could afford; that was too cold, too sharp for me.

Nakada hadn't done anything to me.

And there's another, more pragmatic point. Blackmailers tend to have a short life expectancy. What I'd taken, she could afford. It was no problem. We could draw up a nice, clear, binding contract without ever saying what I was selling her, and she could be pretty sure that I wouldn't come back for more.

But if I'd gone for money, how could she know that? What good would a contract be? People get illogical when money comes into the picture. She might worry about whether I'd come back for more, whether people might trace my money back to her and wonder what I'd done for it—any number of things, until one day I was back on the dayside, or maybe in a ditch somewhere with pseudo-plankton growing on my tongue.

And she hadn't done anything to me.

If it had been Orchid or Lee or Rigmus, if they had Nakada's sort of money, things might have been different. They owed me, just as I still owed Mishima. But I knew how much they had tucked away, and it wasn't enough to tempt me yet. I knew that if I took all of it, they'd find a way to get me—they'd be cornered, and cornered vermin aren't reasonable about these things. If I left enough for them, there wouldn't be enough to be worth the trouble.

I don't know, maybe there would. If I took a piece off the top of all eight shares, I could put together my fare off-planet—but I'd have eight bitter enemies, all of them also bound for Prometheus.

I don't know. I didn't sit down and work out all the ups and downs. I went by instinct, same as I usually do, and I didn't blackmail anyone.

But I didn't know how to explain that to Mishima.

He didn't call back. I didn't have to explain anything.

I did have something to do, though. I'd done my job; it was time to get paid. Zar Pickens owed me a hundred and five credits.

Reaching him by com was clearly hopeless. I called a cab.

Chapter Twenty

THE WEST END STANK. I HADN'T REALLY NOTICED IT before, but it stank—an ugly, organic smell, a composite of a hundred different things.

Sunlight sparked from the tops of the towers, brighter than ever, and I winced at the sight of it.

I reached the address Pickens had given me; the signaller was out, so I knocked on the wall and shrieked, "Anyone home?"

An overweight woman leaned out a window. "Whaddaya want?" she shouted back.

"I'm looking for Zar Pickens," I said.

"Well, you won't find him here," she said. "He moved back east about two days ago, after he got his job back. Those machines they got to replace him couldn't take the work and all broke down. What did you want him for?"

"He owes me money," I said. "Or someone does."

She looked down at me. "Hey, you're that detective he hired, aren't you?"

"Yeah," I said. "Carlisle Hsing, that's me. And I did the job, too. I found out who bought this place, and I have a contract that says you stay rent-free until sunrise—when I get my money."

She stared. "Well, shit," she said. "*I* don't have it."

"Who does? Where can I get it?"

"Shit, *I* don't know." She ducked back in, then popped back out. "But hey, thanks for taking care of it!"

I knew, right then and there, that I was going to get stiffed for the bill—at least until Orchid and Rigmus came around again, which I had already made sure they weren't going to do.

I wasn't about to go back to them and say, "Hey, boys, one more rent run, please, so I can collect my fee." They'd have laughed themselves sick. Hell, they'd have gone, and I'd have gotten my money—but it wasn't worth it. I wasn't going to let them know I got stiffed.

I walked on, prowled on, really, cruising through the West End talking to squatters.

Nobody knew where Pickens was. Nobody knew anything about my fee. Nobody knew anything.

I gave it about ninety minutes, then said the hell with it and called a cab and went home.

I ran Pickens through the city directory and got an address. I put through a call.

He answered.

"Hello, Mis' Pickens," I said.

"Oh, hello, Mis' Hsing," he said, and I could see he was nervous.

"I've got a contract on file here that might interest you. It's an agreement not to evict squatters from property in the West End."

He looked even more nervous, and it took him two tries to say, "What's that got to do with me?"

"Mis' Pickens," I said. "This is what you hired me to get. I got it. You owe me a hundred and five credits."

"Not *me*," he said. "Hey, Hsing, it's not *me*. I'm not even out there anymore. I'm working again; I've got a room here in the burbs where the sun don't shine. I'm no squatter."

"You're the one that hired me, though."

"No, lady, I'm not, either. I was the messenger, that's all."

"Yeah, well, then let me give you a message, messenger. I've got what you wanted. I damn near got killed getting it, and it's cost me one hell of a lot more than the lousy hundred credits you gave me as a down payment. *Somebody* owes me some money."

"Hey, Hsing, it wasn't me, I swear it. Look, I'll go back out there when I've got a free off-shift; I'll tell them, and they'll pay, all right?"

"Oh, right," I said, and I exited.

I figured I might get money a few hours after dawn, if I was lucky. I was mad as hell, and just to annoy myself still more I ran up an account on the case.

Com charges. Cabfare. Drinks at the Manhattan. Medical bills. The cost of one spy-eye. The cost of the bullet I used to shoot it down.

I didn't know how to figure the cost of that murdered cab, the one that was weathering away on the dayside, since it had owned itself. But at least, by god, no matter how lousy I felt about it, that wasn't really my fault. I put it in a separate category, off to the side.

That muscle I'd borrowed from Mishima hadn't come free, I was sure. I estimated what I owed on that.

Even without the cab, without the eye, without the medical bills, it came to a lot more than two hundred and five credits—and I'd only gotten a hundred on account.

With everything figured in, cab and all, it was almost half a megabuck.

I was sitting there staring at that when the com beeped. I punched, and the screen tucked the figures down at the bottom, out of the way, and showed me Sayuri Nakada.

"Hello, Mis' Nakada," I said, hiding the fact that I was seriously puzzled and a good bit worried by the sight of her. "What can I do for you?"

She didn't bother with any polite preliminaries. "Who the hell is this man Mishima?" she demanded.

"Jim Mishima?" I asked.

"That's the one," she agreed. "He says he's your partner."

I saw it all pretty clearly. I hadn't blackmailed her, so Mishima had decided to take care of it himself.

"We aren't exactly partners," I said, "except maybe on a trial basis. I owe him a lot of money—a *lot* of money, and other debts as well. I agreed to work it off as his partner, but we haven't settled the details. Why?"

"He knows about that business we discussed," she said.

"Yeah, I know," I told her. "He tapped my com."

"You didn't tell him?"

"Not intentionally."

"Look, Hsing, if it's that easy to tap your com, maybe you ought to do something about it. I thought we had a deal."

"We do," I said. "I'll take care of it; I've already cleared everything out of active memory. Mishima got to it before I did that, and I'd let him work on my security because of this partnership thing. The information's safe now—at least on *my* system."

"Yes, and what about *his*?"

"What about it?"

"Are you going to clear it out?"

"No," I said. "I can't. I'm sorry."

"You said—look, *is* he your partner or isn't he?"

I blinked, and considered that. "No, he isn't."

"You don't feel any special attachment to him? He's not under your protection?"

That was an odd way of putting it, I thought. "I owe him a lot," I said.

I knew that wasn't what she was after. I knew what she had in mind.

"That's all?"

I hesitated, but finally I said, "That's all."

I knew what I was doing—but Mishima had brought it on himself. He should have known better. He'd gotten involved uninvited again, and this was once too often.

I knew, back when I got that skimmer at the Starshine Palace, that Mishima made mistakes, didn't always see the obvious.

I owed him, but that didn't make me his keeper. I wasn't responsible for his mistakes.

And I'd never *asked* him to come out looking for me or pay my medical bills.

"That's what I wanted to know," she said, and I caught her just before she exited.

"Hey," I said. "I won't stop you; you do what you need to. But please, remember that I owe him, and that I can't pay a debt to a memory."

She looked at me out of the screen, then nodded. "I'll try," she said.

Then the screen blanked for a second, and the numbers from the bottom surged up to fill it again.

I erased them. I didn't want to think about it.

The thought of warning Mishima crossed my mind, but I decided against it. Nakada wouldn't appreciate it—and he'd brought it on himself. I'd warned him, and he'd said he could take care of himself. Here was his chance.

The thought of calling the cops also crossed my mind;

after all, I had plenty of evidence against Orchid and Rigmus, and enough against Lee and the others to at least start an investigation.

I decided against that, too. I wasn't feeling suicidal. I knew that if I ever brought the cops into it, with Nakada on the other side I'd have the deck stacked against me. And most of my com evidence about the scam Orchid and Lee were running on Nakada had been acquired illegally. If I ever turned it over to anyone, I would be signing my own reconstruction order.

And this doesn't even mention that the casino cops work under an IRC service contract.

So I didn't call the cops, about Mishima or anything else.

It was much later, when I was eating a bowl of rice and considering bed and staring at the negative balance in my primary credit account, that the com beeped again.

I touched, and 'Chan appeared.

"Carlie," he said. "I thought you ought to know. Big Jim Mishima's been arrested."

"What's it to me?" I asked.

"Oh, come on, Carlie," he said. "Don't give me that. I was there in the hospital. I saw you when he bought you in."

"All right," I said. "Who's arrested him? What's the charge?"

"The casino cops picked him up for cheating, at the New York. A security unit broke his jaw, and the management has him under heavy privacy seal. I hear that as victim's privilege they want to wipe his memory and files for the last ten days."

That made sense. It was something that I could live with. I didn't like it, but I could live with it. It would make everything simple. I nodded.

"Carlie," 'Chan said, "what's going on? Is this something of yours?"

I shook my head. "'Chan," I said, "if it is, do you really want to be involved?"

He considered that. "No."

"That's what I thought," I said. Something occurred to me. "Hey," I asked, "how'd you hear about it?"

"It was on the casino grapevine," he said. "I'm at the Ginza now, and we get a lot of feed from the New York."

"Oh." I couldn't think of anything more to say. 'Chan just stared out of the screen at me.

"Thanks for calling," I finally said.

"No problem," he replied. "Carlie, are you in trouble? Is there anything I can do?'

"No," I said. "Thanks, but I'm okay." I exited.

But I wasn't sure I was okay. I wasn't sure at all.

Sayuri Nakada had removed one threat and done a fairly neat job of it—but I was still around. Mishima's employees were still around, too. She'd started removing enemies; could she really stop with just one?

And did I really want to leave her free to buy up Nightside City? Did I want to risk the crew at the Ipsy trying a little demonstration blast, despite their promise? Could I be sure that Orchid and Rigmus wouldn't decide to remove me, ITEOD files or no ITEOD files?

Did I really want to stay in Nightside City, in my rundown little office in the burbs, taking two-buck jobs from the dregs of the city, hanging out at Lui's because I wasn't welcome anywhere better, ignored by my friends back in the Trap and by my father dreaming eternally in Trap Under—just sitting and waiting for the sun?

I was sick of it all. I had known all along that I had to get off Epimetheus eventually, and I decided that the time had come. I could still beat the rush. I didn't have the fare, but I knew just what to do about that.

I didn't want to try blackmail—Big Jim Mishima, with his broken jaw to keep him from talking, had tried that. I couldn't very well go to the cops. But I had information to sell, and I knew where to sell it. Mishima had told me.

I did a little work on the com, pulling stuff back into active memory and packaging things up neatly on a pocket datatab; when I was finished with that, I put all my best working software on another pocket tab.

After that, I erased my whole system, right back down to the landlord's lousy original housekeeping programs. I was done with it; even if something went wrong, I was done with it all.

Then I called a cab and went down to the street. I took the shoulderbag with the HG-2 in it.

The cab was a Daewoo; I'd never seen one before. I took it as an omen, of sorts, that new things were happening, that my life was about to change. I got in out of the wind and told it to take me to the New York—the business entrance on the roof, not the street.

It dropped me there, in the middle of a shimmering holo that was half siren, half demon, and I buzzed at the door.

The scanners gave me the once over and asked my business.

"I have an important message," I said. "For Yoshio Nakada. About his great-granddaughter Sayuri."

The scanners locked in on me. The door didn't open.

"Ask Mis' Vo," I said. Old Vijay Vo was still the manager of the New York. "He'll know whether Mis' Nakada will want to hear about this."

I waited, and after a moment the door opened. A floater hung inside, blocking my way. "Leave the gun," it said.

I gave it the HG-2, and it gave me a receipt and let me

pass. A line of golden flitterbugs formed an arrow and led the way.

The manager's office was done in dark red plush; the ceiling shimmered with red and gold field effects. Vo sat behind his desk. I stood.

"You ought to know who I am," I told Vo.

"I do, Mis' Hsing," he said.

"And you know I've been investigating Sayuri Nakada."

He nodded.

"Well, I think that Yoshio Nakada will be very interested in what I found out, and I want to talk to him. You must have a line to him here."

"We have a line to his office, yes. You can't just tell me, and trust me to act accordingly?"

I shook my head. "I'm sorry, Mis' Vo," I said. "But this is a matter of vital interest to Nakada Enterprises and the Nakada family, and I hope to earn a fat fee out of it. I don't know you. I don't know how you stand in relation to either Yoshio or Sayuri. I know nothing at all against you, but no, I can't, at present, trust you."

He leaned back and watched me thoughtfully for a few seconds.

"All right," he said. He was a man of decision; I appreciated that. I'd also expected it, from what I'd heard of him.

"You understand the com delay, don't you?" he asked me.

I nodded. "How much is it at present?"

"About twelve minutes each way, a little over twenty-three round-trip. Prometheus isn't too far away just now."

That might not seem to far to him, since he was used to it, but I realized I was about to start the slowest conversation of my life. You can't put a message on a Wheeler drive unless you put it on a ship, and you can't hold a conversation by ship. I was limited to light speed.

I nodded again. "All right," I said.

He turned me over to the flitterbugs again, and they led me out of his office and into the New York's holy of holies, or of holos anyway, a bare little room with holos on all six sides.

One of Vo's assistants was there. She jacked in for a minute to put me through.

I'd expected them to keep the line open full-time, but I suppose the power bill would have been ridiculous.

She unplugged. "You'll get his office, but probably not the old man himself. It's all yours."

She turned and left me alone—but I didn't doubt that Vo was listening somewhere. I didn't mind; as long as I got through to Yoshio Nakada's people on Prometheus I figured I was all set.

The holo signalled that I was transmitting, and I began talking.

I wanted to get as much in each message as possible—to keep those twenty-three minute delays to a minimum.

"My name is Carlisle Hsing," I said. "I'm a free-lance private investigator here in Nightside City. I recently had a case that led me, unexpectedly, to investigate Sayuri Nakada. I believe the information I acquired may be of great interest to her family and her financial backers. The client who originally hired me for the job has refused to pay my bill, so that I feel justified in offering the information for sale on the open market. My asking price is five hundred thousand credits. If you accept this, I'll include an account showing that more than ninety percent of that is to cover legitimate expenses incurred in the investigation. The rest is mostly needed to pay my fare from Nightside City to Prometheus, since I believe my life is in danger here. I also ask for protection once I'm there, if it's necessary. This information may lead to several felony prosecutions. It may also remind you of certain episodes in Sayuri Nakada's life prior to her departure from Prometheus. And I hope very much that it will prevent a large waste of money, and consequent damage to the Nakada reputation. End of message."

Then I sat, and I waited.

Twenty-three minutes later the wall in front of me vanished, and I had a view of an office on Prometheus, done in slick white and chrome. A window showed me a rich blue sky, and I realized I was calling the dayside there—but that didn't mean much. The day on Prometheus doesn't burn the skin from your back or the sight from your eyes. It doesn't last forever. It's nine hours of pleasant warmth and light.

A handsome woman looked at me from that office, listening to the words I'd spoken, and then said, "Please wait here, Mis' Hsing; I don't have the authority to act on this, but I'll get someone who does."

I won't drag you through it step by step. I was locked in that little holoroom for eleven hours, time enough to see the sky outside that window darken and sprinkle itself with stars and even a small moon. I spoke to four different people. I never did speak to Yoshio himself; I only got as far as an aide named Ziyang Subbha. He approved my request, not even dickering very seriously about the price. He authorized a draft against the New York for 492,500 credits.

I plugged my tab into the transmitter and sent it all, everything I had, everything that had happened since Zar Pickens beeped from my doorstep, everything I've just told you, with all the documentation.

Then I got my draft, put it on my card, got my gun back, and went home. I packed up everything I wanted; there wasn't much. I paid all my bills, including everything I owed Mishima—though with his memory wiped he might never know what it was all about. I hesitated over the price of the wrecked cab, and then put half of it in the account of the Q.Q.T. cab that had coded my card for a tip, and kept the other half for myself. I thought about stopping at Lui's Tavern for some good-byes, but decided not to bother; I admitted to myself that I'd never really been much more than another face in the crowd there. I thought about calling a few programs that knew me well, but decided against that, too—software doesn't miss people the way humans do, and it gets used to the way all we humans are constantly moving about, in and out of contact. I left a message for 'Chan, but I didn't send it directly; I put it on delay, to be delivered after twenty-four hours. I didn't want to have any family arguments about what I was doing.

There wasn't anybody else I wanted to call, so I didn't. I shut down every system in the place and got my bags.

And then I headed for the port.

I didn't know for sure what would happen in the city, but I could guess. Sayuri would be spanked and sent home. Orchid and Rigmus and the rest would be sent for reconstruction. Mishima would carry on, looking for the big break, probably wondering what the hell he had gotten messed up in during his lost time. The Nakada family had the money and power to see to all of that.

Nightside City would go on for a while. The miners would come in and gamble away the pay they spent their lives earning. The tourists would come and gawk and gamble. The city itself would go on. And in time, right on schedule, the sun would rise. The long night would be over, and the city would die.

One thing I did know for sure.

I wouldn't be there to see it.

ABOUT THE AUTHOR

LAWRENCE WATT-EVANS was born and raised in eastern Massachusetts, the fourth of six children in a house full of books. Both parents were inveterate readers, and both enjoyed science fiction; he grew up reading anything handy, including a wide variety of speculative fiction. His first attempts at writing SF were made at the age of seven.

After surviving twelve years of public schooling, he followed in the footsteps of father and grandfather and attended Princeton University. Less successful than his ancestors, he left without a degree after two attempts.

Being qualified for no other enjoyable work—he had discovered working in ladder factories, supermarkets, or fast-food restaurants to be something less than enjoyable—he began trying to sell his writing between halves of his college career, with a notable lack of success. After his final departure from Princeton, however, he produced *The Lure of the Basilisk*, which sold readily, beginning his career as a full-time writer. *Nightside City* is his twelfth novel; of the twelve, six are science fiction and six are fantasy.

He married in 1977, has two children, and lives in the Maryland suburbs of Washington, D.C.